Percy H. Fitzgerald

Fatal zero, a diary kept at Homburg

Vol. 1

Percy H. Fitzgerald

Fatal zero, a diary kept at Homburg
Vol. 1

ISBN/EAN: 9783337125103

Printed in Europe, USA, Canada, Australia, Japan

Cover: Foto ©Andreas Hilbeck / pixelio.de

More available books at **www.hansebooks.com**

FATAL ZERO,

A Diary kept at Homburg.

IN TWO VOLUMES.

VOL. I.

LONDON:

TINSLEY BROTHERS, 18, CATHERINE STREET, STRAND.

1869.

LONDON :
SAVILL, EDWARDS AND CO., PRINTERS, CHANDOS STREET,
COVENT GARDEN.

TO

D. O. S.

O softest glades, and balmy morning airs,
 Green lanes that wind, and many a chequered Alley ;
 With solemn Taunus shelt'ring all the valley—
Here surely man may lose his heavy cares.
 Yet here the boiling heart, the raging eye,
 The pulse that stops upon the fatal call
 Of Red and Black, and leap of whirling Ball,
 Scenes of dark horror that I fain would fly—
Fly but for one sweet face that holds me bound,
 And her bright presence makes it Holy ground.

May, 1869.

FATAL ZERO.

CHAPTER I.

Datchley, Monday, August the First, 186–.
—Another day of agony, and of acting.
Soon all must be stopped. This cannot go
on. Here is my last day of absence from the
bank, and I am not one bit better. They
have been only too indulgent. But what
can they do? They must have their work
done, and already the directors are com-
plaining, up in the London office.

A hundred and fifty pounds a year,
and that darling of mine, Dora—the chil-

dren—all depending on me. If I lost this situation, what would become of us? And yet I must lose it. My fingers can scarcely feel this pen, and the trembling characters swim before my eyes. As I write on, the paper seems to rise up like waves of a huge white sea, and suffuse my very pupils. What am I to do?

There, my darling has just gone out with the usual question, "How do you feel now, dear? You are stronger after this rest, are you not?" And I falsely say "Yes!" How can I pain her—she suffers more than I do. Oh, what folly and infatuation to have brought her into this state of life! I should have stood by, and let her marry that man, who would have at least maintained her in comfort; but my own selfishness would not let me. He might have turned out a good husband. Though he was not a good man, she must have made him one. But my selfishness must sacrifice her to myself. Just like us all!

There! I open a book—a favourite one of mine—"The Following of Christ," and read a sentence; up rises the page to my eyes like a huge wave of foam; a faint buzzing begins in my ears, and swells into the roar of a great sea. What *does* all this mean? What can be coming? God preserve my senses! Or can this be a punishment that I have deserved? Yet the doctor proceeds with his cant, "A little rest is all that is wanted—you must give up work." How smoothly they say these things—so complacently! And pray will you, sir, feed her, feed them, pay the rent? No! so far from that, his greedy eye is wandering to her gentle delicate little fingers, which by the divine Aladdin's Lamp a dear devoted girl contrives to find, have hold of what will satisfy him. We men can find for ourselves readily enough, but *they* find for others. There—there, I must stop.

That cruel fellow, Maxwell, the manager, has been twice here, in these three days. A cold, hard, cruel, vindictive man. He says he supposes I am suffering, " as I say so," but really he cannot see what is wrong with me. With difficulty restraining myself, I ask him, Does he suppose I am counter-feiting, or that the doctor was counterfeit-ing? He answers in his insolent way, that what he supposed privately did not much bear on the matter; the question was how was the bank to get its work done. I must see that they could not go on paying high salaries to invalids. He had his duty to the board and shareholders. I was either very sick, or only a little sick. If the former, I had better resign—if the latter, I had better make an exertion and return to my work. They really could give me no longer than to-morrow at furthest.

Poor Dora shrinks from this cruel sentence as if she were standing in the dock with a child in her arms.

" Oh, Mr. Maxwell," she cries, " you will not be so cruel!" He gave her a savage look.

" Ah! that is the word they have for me through the town. Mr. Maxwell, the hard man—a griping, cruel man. I do my duty, Mrs. Austen; and let every one else, whether they are ladies and gentlemen or no, do theirs."

Lady and gentleman!—that was our crime. He never forgave that. He had once swept the very bank offices, so the story went. He had no religion but money and figures. He had never been seen once in a place of worship, and one of the clerks once saw a cheap translation of the infidel

Renan on his table. Yet whatever he does to us, I can pray for him to the indulgent Lord of all, and I shall get Dora to do the same. There again, I must stop. This agitation makes me forget for a few seconds that I cannot write.

CHAPTER II.

Tuesday.—At last it has all broken down. I knew when the morning came that it would be so—though we all cling to the notion that " to-morrow morning" will bring a change. I dare not go to the office. I am quite helpless. She sees it, and knows the miserable night I have passed. I have sent to Maxwell, to the bank. He has cruelly warned me, that on the day after to-morrow they will officially call upon me to resign. Then what will be done! . . . Only one thing—Heaven's will.

Three o'clock.—Mr. Stanhope, the curate, has just gone. Lord Langton has fallen

from his horse, and they have got down Sir
Duncan Denison, the great London doctor
—a good man and a charitable man—and
Mr. Stanhope has brought him on to me.
But such a remedy! I could have laughed,
but for her sad face. " My good friend, I
tell you seriously, no tricks will do here.
You are in a bad way at this moment; and
I must assure you solemnly, your only
chance is the German waters, and listen,
one special one of those German waters—
Homburg, is the only thing to save you.
I snatched a man from the jaws, nay, from
the throat of death, this year, by pack-
ing him off. You should go to-morrow
morning."

A fine remedy, and a precious one, truly.
Maxwell comes in as the doctor is here, and
Dora passionately tells him what has been
said.

He listens coolly and civilly.

"With that I have nothing to do. We have to begin making out our report to-night, and, I can tell you, are not going to take on fresh hands to swell the expenses. The best thing you can do—and I advise you as manager—is to resign at once. I have another man ready for the place, and I daresay it could be arranged that a quarter's salary could be got in some way, as a bonus, with which you could take your expedition."

"And leave *them* to starve! What do you suppose is to become of them? Are they to be turned out on the road? Has your bank, your board of blood-suckers, no heart, no soul?"

"Board of blood-suckers, sir!—the Associated Bank that sort of thing! God bless me, no!" said Sir Duncan, who had been silent. "I attend at least two of the directors, as honest and soft fellows as ever signed a cheque. They're not the fellows to suck anybody's blood—unless at least, they do it in private."

" They are men of business, sir," said Maxwell, " and do their duty to the bank and the shareholders. Only that he seems ill, it would be my duty to report this language."

They all left us, Sir Duncan saying,

" My poor fellow, I am really sorry for you! I see the difficulty. Something may turn up."

We, however, were calm. As I said before, I had taught Dora whom to turn to in these straits, and bade her pray for even Maxwell. On myself I find a sort of insensibility coming, I suppose from illness. And yet I have great vitality and life, and if there was a crisis or purpose before me, could shake all off for a time.

CHAPTER III.

Four o'clock!—What ungrateful creatures
we are! Oh, to an ever-bountiful Providence be all praise and glory, and honour
and gratitude! It seems like a miracle;
but confidence, somehow, never failed me.
A telegram lies before me, from the directors in London. A note from Maxwell, at
the same time. He would not come himself
to tell us good news, though he came so
often before, to gloat over our miseries.
But I shall find out more of his treachery.
Still I am so joyous, so supremely happy,
I can be angry with no one. Mr. Barnard,
who is a director, but who has been away

on the Continent, has come down himself. He has seen and told me the plan—leave of absence—recreation—peace—quiet—and *I am not to resign!* Oh, happy change! I feel as in a dream!

Five o'clock.—There is yet more happiness to set down. I can hardly write these words—not from sickness, but from excitement. It is all settled, and I go, not in the morning, but to-night—this very night. Heaven is very good — too good! This was the way. Only an hour ago Mr. Barnard came in here—his knock made me tremble.

"So you are ill?" he said, it seemed with sternness. "Well, this cannot go on. You will lose your situation; you know the bank must have its work done."

" I know it, sir," I said.

" And so this Sir Duncan says nothing short of Homburg will do for you. A first-class watering-place, and an expensive journey—for a bank clerk! Well, well!"

Dora was in a flood of tears. " Oh, but he will die, sir!" she said, passionately.

"No he wont," he said, with a sudden change in manner—"or, at least, if he does, it shall be his own fault. Come, he shall go, and at once too."

My dear gave a scream. I felt the colour in my own face. He sat down and set out details of this miraculous deliverance.

Here was the plan, and I do recognise in it one more proof of that actual guidance of Providence—that positive interference in our affairs here below. Oh, how unworthy, I say again, are we of such goodness! Our bank, it seems, in London, has a good many Jew directors, and has been trying to get a little foreign business in the way of agency. A rich Frankfurt merchant, whom he knew, was anxious to buy an estate in England, for which Barnard was trustee. It was a small one, but he fancied the situation and the house. The writings were prepared; and a solicitor was going out to have them executed, receive the money, and make other arrangements, when Mr. Barnard conceived this idea of substituting me for the solicitor.

" You shall have your expenses there and back, and handsome ones, too, out of which you can squeeze a fortnight's keep. But you must be back within the month; no shirking, mind, for I am your warranty, and get well, too; make use of every hour; for if you lose this chance, we cannot promise you another. And now see here—let me give you a piece of advice. You are a young man: you have been nearly all your life in a country town, and have not seen much of the world. You have good religious instincts. But you will see many things abroad that will shock you. I know those places well. Now take my advice—don't concern yourself at all with what you may see—just busy yourself with the one object of your expedition—that is, of getting all the relaxation you can, and getting well."

" Oh, indeed he will, dear Mr. Barnard," said Dora, eagerly, the hot tears still glistening in her eyes.

" Of course I need not warn you against what goes on there. You are a poor man, and, in matter of pecuniary ' Breeks,' would be as unprofitable as any Highlander."

This was his little joke, and almost as of course, we laughed.

Was this a morsel of the bread of dependency? But he was a good man, and it was only his way. So God bless him for his kindness.

"See," I say to my darling, "what did I say yesterday? Never lose trust. You were a little desponding. You believed that all was lost. My heart never for a moment faltered."

"I know that, dearest. But you will do as he says. Not worry yourself about their wicked doings. You are so good, and so pious. I know it will hurt your dear heart."

"But he says," I answer, "that I have been brought up in a country town, and know nothing of the world. Would to Heaven I did not. He believes the world is only to be known by hurrying over railways, and strange cities, as if we had not all the great Book of the Human Heart, ready wide open before us. But he is good and noble, and Heaven bless him and reward him."

He has gone. A case with all the papers

and a letter of instruction, has just come up. A clerk who brought them counted down fifty golden sovereigns. It seems like a dream. Dora danced round them and actually kissed one. If she were only coming, my love and guardian angel; but we cannot compass that! Surely it will be only for one month, and I shall come back to her, happy and strong, and able to work for her and our children again. Is it a dream? It is like a wish in a Fairy Tale.

Ten o'clock.—As we sat this evening in a state almost of rapture—for indeed it has all the air of a supernatural deliverance— our good clergyman, Mr. Bulmer, was ushered in. How warmly he caught my hand!

" My dear friends," he said, " how de- lighted I am at this good news! Going abroad is the only thing for you. It will cure and make a man of you. Leave all ·

cares behind you, at home in the lumber-
room, and fling yourself into a round of
rational and healthful joys."

"Oh, indeed he intends it," said dear
Dora, as though she were making a promise for some erring brother, who had promised to reform, and turn over a new leaf.
"He has promised not to open a book, or
think of what is disagreeable, or worry himself.   And we can depend on his promise."

"That's right.   And what part have
you chosen?   Switzerland — Tyrol?   No?
Paris?"

"Homburg," I said.   "There are waters
there; and the curious life there will be the
more entertaining and curious—since I am
bound over to consider that——"

"That is, this gambling place.   I don't
see why you should pick it out.   I should
say, it could be profitable neither to soul
nor to body."

"He did not pick it out," says Dora, eagerly. "The doctor ordered him." Our good clergyman is of the severe Evangelical school, and naturally takes a stern view of these things. I dare say he is right.

"I knew something of the chaplain there —a good, zealous man, who has worked hard to stem the current, when I might have gone down comfortably and cozily on the surface. He told me a good deal about it. But now, do you know what I am thinking? It is not so much the place, as the person——"

"The person!" repeated Dora, mystified.

"Yes. No one should run into needless risks. I dare say I would not trust myself —or rather, I would safely—because I am old and case-hardened. I had a parish in London once. The work was too much for me. But you see, he"—motioning to me— "has scarcely ever been out of a country

2—2

town. He is more or less unsophisticated, and all this sort of thing coming on an untrained mind"—here he shook his head—"I don't quite like it, Mrs. Dora."

"But he's not untrained. He is so clever, and so——"

"Hush, Dora, dear! You make me blush. There is something in what Mr. Bulmer says—though I am hardly so raw as he thinks——"

"Raw! Folly. I speak bluntly, you know; but I mean well. What I fear is this. He *is* a clever fellow; and you naturally think yourself one, Master Austen, having a nice wife to tell you so every day. And I will add to it, Mrs. Dora, he is quite as good, as he is clever. I have not a more religious, or more earnest man in my flock. And that's why I am anxious about him."

My Dora looked round with pride at

this commendation, which she would have gone forth, and had emblazoned in gold, and hung up. I only smiled.

"You are very kind, Mr. Bulmer; and it is very kind of you to say so. I do mean to be good soon, especially when my health is restored. Besides," I added, good-humouredly, "for the sake of this bank I ought to try and sharpen these poor raw wits of mine, and learn a little of the world."

"He doesn't forgive me that stupid speech of mine," said he, laughing very heartily. "And it *was* stupid. But see, my dear boy, don't mind the rubbish these doctors tell you about waters, and the like. Go to the noble mountains of Switzerland. A week with those grand councillors will do you more true good, than months in the fetid miasma of the gaming rooms."

"I am sure they would," I said; "but,

alas! I am not free to choose. I have business given me to transact."

"Well, you will do very well; and this dear girl will keep praying for you; though I dare say she thinks me an old croaker. No matter. It is no harm for you to be humble, my dear boy, or to think yourself weak. Good-by, and Heaven bless you!"

He always did speak his mind—a good, well-meaning man, that I respect from my soul, with an interest in his. I am so tranquil and happy now at my good fortune, that I could bring myself to thank him for his kind and fatherly advice, which the foolish or self-opinioned would resent.

"My darling, I see is not quite pleased."

"You, with your cleverness and observation! Why, I only said last week that, if you choose, you could preach a better sermon any Sunday."

"Hush! rank heresy, darling! Better

than the parson of the parish?" Ill as I was, I could not help laughing at this test of my pet's. "I fear a very inferior nature could beat our good Bulmer at preaching."

"He has never been abroad himself but once," she said, "so he can scarcely know much about what he is condemning: though, indeed, he is very kind—and has been so kind."

"No better man breathing, and I am obliged to him for his interest. Still I am obliged to go and face these appalling dangers. Heaven grant it may do me good! If it should not, I tremble to think what is to become of us."

"Why, are you not better this moment?" she said, almost passionately; "or am I tiring you?"

I said, "Yes." There is no harm in such a little fiction.

Eleven o'clock.—There, this day is over,

and I am now sitting at the fire, bewildered, yet in a sweet bewilderment. It is nearly midnight, and I feel as though I had been rescued from a fire—from drowning—reprieved from execution, life seems so exquisitely enjoyable. O, how grateful I ought to be! and so indeed I am; for I am to leave to-morrow evening.

Dora has just gone, after we have talked for hours—talked over everything; over the events of the day, over that good Mr. Barnard who has done so much, and done it so delicately. Heaven bless him, for ever and ever more, as indeed we prayed, and prayed long together. She—my darling —said in her natural way, that it must be so utterly bewildering to go forth so suddenly into a far-off strange land, among strangers, and without a friend. Alas! yes. But I may not take her. And yet, as I said, it seems as bewildering for her to be

left behind, alone, for the first time since
our marriage—no one to consult—no one
to turn to—no one to advise her. I know
not what she will do, but have promised to
write—write nearly every day. It will be
like speaking to her.

My poor, poor child! I forget my own
sufferings as I think of her. I leave her
behind unprotected. Good, kind Mr. Barnard—he has done enough, he will think,
and *should* not do more. Besides, his is a
nature for the good, noble, coarse work of
charity; he does not understand the delicate nerves and fibres of her nature, exquisitely fine-spun. A cold speech scares her,
as a rude and rough one would another.
There is that cruel Maxwell, the manager,
who never spared debtor, and would wish
she were his debtor. Left to herself, too,
for the first time, even for so short a space
as a month, with the gossips of this place

clustering round obtrusively—who knows what stories, what influences! But this is all morbid. Yet I could not help drawing the dear child towards me, and giving her a little advice against these dangers.

"Dearest," I said, "when I shall have gone out into the world, as you say, you will be left here alone, and unprotected, for the first time."

"Not alone," she says, prettily, "for I shall think of you so much, that I shall see you nearly as well as I do now."

(In her there is always this under-current of sentiment,—and such sweet sentiment.)

"Alas," I say, "that will be but a poor protection! My poor unworthy image, how will *that* shield you?"

"Yes, it will," she answered quickly, "if I know that it is getting a strong image."

"But how will you carry on the battle of life? *Who* will talk to the butcher and baker, for that *is* the battle of life after all. Ah, dear, you were made for the smooth swards of life, not for the high roads."

"I prefer the high roads," says my sweet child, confidently, "and you shall see how well I can walk."

Now I thought at this moment, I would give that dear soul a *little* caution, just for her own sake. She could not see the risks; it was the first time in her life, she had stood alone. Her father, mother, and doting family had done all for her, before *I* came. Since then, with this wretched illness growing on me I had done all. *I* had faced butcher, baker, and the rest. *I* had kept out the forward intruders—even the half-patron, who wished to be considered a friend, but who would honour us with visits, more frequent than were usual with merely disinterested friendship. I knew how to deal with such firmly, yet without

bluntness. There was that young Honour-
able, so solicitous about my health. He
perfectly understood me, though my sweet,
innocent Dora did not.

So, ill as I am, I cannot help speaking to
her with a gentle warning, and telling her
the truth. "My pet," I say, "the strongest
of us is but a child, *when once we begin to
think ourselves strong.* You never heard
that from Mr. Bulmer's pulpit. Yet it is
worth much more than some of the conventional truths, which, good and well-
meaning man as he is, he believes to be the
best that he can hold out to us. That is
what I feared for my darling. But she
will pray, she will promise me *that*—pray
for strength, and against all temptation. If
I only was certain of that, I should have
comfort on my weary travels."

Promise me that! She would have promised me the world ten times over! So

gentle, so confiding, so full of her own utmost helplessness! Indeed I feel a pang now when I think of my doubts, yet still it is a responsibility, and a prayer for strength can do her no harm. Heaven knows it is but for her good, and comes but from excessive love. How blessed, how happy I am, on this night. I have the old pains, the old "swimming" still, but I do not heed them. There is release and salvation at hand, and I feel like some one condemned to penal servitude years ago, and now suddenly released. My portmanteau lies there —packed—strapped—like a bluff companion muffled and buttoned up, and seems to nod jollily at me, and say, "I am ready when you are!"

Wednesday, London, Charing Cross Hotel.
—Bore the journey wonderfully, absolutely getting better already. This comes from all hope dancing before my eyes. No

ledger this morning—My heart is bounding within me. So curious this great gorgeous chamber all gold, where a hundred people are taking breakfast. I can hear the screaming of the engine close by—My train—yes, in ten minutes. Delightful all this excitement. It is new life—a bright sunny day—the bustling crowds going by —the gay look of everything, and the pleasant journey all before me.

CHAPTER IV.

Brussels, Six p.m.—Such a day as it has been—a delicious sea—happy travellers—charming green fields, and the strange look of Ostend, the first foreign place I have ever seen. All red tiles and potsherds, it seemed to me, at a distance. Then the white quays and yellow houses. Then the trains through the pleasant Belgian country; the odd faces and dresses, and that singular custom of the guard coming in so mysteriously at the door, when the train is at full speed. What things I shall have to tell darling Dora, and amuse her with! Her name makes my heart low; only this

excitement prevents me thinking of anything dismal. Perhaps I shall write a book
of travels, make a little money, and give it
all to her. And yet having seen so much
already, it does not seem to me, that I have
acquired an ounce more worldly wisdom.
No, my dear friend Mr. Barnard was a little
wrong there.

But this amazing and delicious capital!
It is awe-striking—so solid and splendid—
and the glorious cathedral! Such wealth,
such gorgeousness to be in the world, which
we scarcely even dream of. The trees in
the streets, the people sitting out and taking coffee, the splendid carriages, and all
with such a grand and noble air of stateli-
ness. I have noted a thousand things to
tell Dora when I return. I feel getting
stronger every moment, and a quarter of
an hour ago actually read an English paper,
without finding the words swimming, and

the paper rising up to my eyes. I posi-. tively think I shall go on to-night.

Friday, Cologne.—A long night in the great roomy carriages, and very comfort- able. A little curtain to draw over the lamp, and the whole left to myself, so I might have been in my own room. Yet I did not get to sleep till nearly one o'clock; not so much from noise or novelty, as from my own thoughts, so much was coming back on me. This was the first time I had been away from home, from Dora; and now that I was at a distance, she, and all that had passed, began to rise before me like pictures. I could see now—like a man walking back to get a good view of a picture—her sweet face in the centre, and what a deal I had gone through to win it for myself! Though she never shall know it, much of what I suffer now is owing to that six years' feverish anxiety. And I.

saved her from him. For a time I did feel some remorse, yet now I do not. It was all for a good end, which, whatever the casuists say, does sometimes justify the means.

Let me think now, as an entertainment, of the first bright day on which I saw her. Some wealthy people, who lived in tolerable state, had "filled their house," as it is called, and had asked me down. I was reluctant to go. In these days—and not unpleasant days were they—I quite lived in the book world, and very pleasant friends I had among them. For as Richard of Bury says, in words that sound like old church bells, "These are the masters that instruct us without rods; if you chide them they do not answer, if you neglect or ill- treat them, they bear no malice. They are always cheerful, sweet-tempered, ready to talk and comfort us, at any hour of night or day."

For them I felt an affection—they seemed to me beautiful, with charming faces, and shall I own it?—some of the prettiest faces of nature when shown to me, appeared to me much as these pretty faces would look on my mouldy treasures. Do I not remember how I used to look out at the world, as from a window, and punctually as the clock struck twelve every night, would put away work, fetch out the best novel of the day, light the soothing cigar, and read for two hours? How enjoyable was this time, almost too exquisite! But the whole was about to collapse like a card house.

How curious this dark country looks, actually "roaring by," with glare and flash from a station—the dull "burr" of the train, and the lights from the row of carriage windows dappling the ground. As I look out I see the small dark figure of the guard creeping along outside. In this situation, in my lonely blue chamber, there is a sort of vacuity for thought, the world is shut out and the pictures of the past pour in . . . .

A railway carriage is like a cell. It is all vacuum, and no objects to distract. It is like the plane on which dissolving views are projected, and I never could entertain myself with my own thoughts so well. I often call up those days—they were so happy—she like a gentle angel, not the soft meek conventional angel, who has a flavour of insipidity, but something so brilliant and attractive. What a time it was.

Was it not a very stately place—quite a new castle, grand stabling, horses and carriages in profusion. As I was shown into the great drawing-room, and received with welcome by the hostess, the guests were all out, shooting, riding, walking, and—so unfortunately, she says—lunch was over. The young ladies were in the garden, where I could go and look for them. Stay; they were coming, and past the mullioned windows, which ran down to the ground, flitted two or three figures, led by a little scarlet cloak. In a second, cheerful voices rang out like music in the hall: the door opened, and *she* came tripping in. I did not see the others. I do not know who they were to this moment; but was it not *then*, my dear foolish Austen, that everything fell in like a house of cards—that the glory passed away from the books for ever, and never returned?

Her name was Dora—a pretty and melodious one. She was small, elegantly made, with dancing eyes, bright sloe-black hair, and a look of refinement about her small features I have never seen in any one else. A great London sculptor so admired that

head, that he begged to be allowed to copy
it for one of his nymphs. She was full of
spirits, and laughter, and delight. I recollect to this moment how I was introduced,
with what a coquettish solemnity she went
through the ceremony, and how, as I
bowed, I felt something whisper to me,
"This, sir, is an important moment for
you . . ."

She was a daughter of a great House in
the neighbourhood. From that hour she
unconsciously entered into my life. She
little thought how her airy figure was to
hover about my study, and of how many
daydreams she was to be the centre. Since
that morning years have gone by; yet
that dull blue cloth before me seems to
open and draw away, and show me that gay
noonday and that " morning room" at ——
Castle, as distinctly as if it were but yesterday. In my pocket-book I have at this

moment her picture, done, not by the fanciful touch of memory, but by, perhaps, the less enduring one of the camera. It is very hard to see by this light. Yes, there she is—a cloud of white sweeping behind her, flowers in her hand—a soft inquiring look, half serious, yet that seems on the verge of breaking into a smile, and spoiling the operator's whole work. So I saw her then, so I see her now. What if I was never to see her again! Am I not in bad health, "broken down," as they call it in their jargon? It is on the cards. Oh, the very notion gives a twist and turn and wrench at my heart! *Lose her for ever!* The last stroke of a passing bell sounds less dismal. But this is too lugubrious.

CHAPTER V.

THERE, the blast again—a flashing and
flaring of lamps, a scream of the whistles,
and we rumble into a blaze of light, with
buffets and offices lit up, and an open line
of sleepy passengers waiting. One fellow
in a white hat invades my blue chamber—
a gross Belgian, with a theatrical portmanteau pushed in before him, and an air as if
he were performing some feat of distinction.
Away flutters her little figure, and from
that moment the charm is broken, clouds of
tobacco-smoke begin, wherein, I suppose—
fitting background—he sees pictures of
his own gross déjeûner à la fourchette, or

dinner, at the Trois Frères. A true beast, that presently grunts and snores, lives but for the present hour, and never lifts up his soul in gratitude or humility. There, he has got out, and I have done with him. I know now the secret of this dislike; he reminded me so of Grainger, the only evil genius I ever encountered in my life, and the evil genius that I vanquished. Rather, grace and strength came to me from above, to aid me to vanquish him.

I see the very street in our little town, on that gay morning when he first appeared. How well I remember our all rushing to the window of the bank, the day the regiment came in—when we heard their music, and I must have seen him—Grainger—walk by, with his sword drawn, at the head of his company, and looked at him, perhaps with admiration. I little dreamed what he was to be towards me later. I thought of their coming with pleasure; it would vary the monotony. I thought of how they would amuse her, perhaps, for whom a country town must be dull indeed. Later, I see soldiers walking about the place, the officers rather fine and contemptuous, for which one could bear them no ill-will, as they had fought and bled for us, and might take little airs. . . .

A cold blast and rush of air, as the conductor has come in once more like a spirit, with a lantern, and wants to see tickets. These interruptions are very tedious and making me perfectly wakeful. . . .

Let me look back again, setting my head, now aching a good deal, against these comfortable cushions. It is not likely that I shall sleep under these strange conditions. I like dwelling on little pictures of that time, and it is an easy and pleasant amusement constructing them.

I next see one of our country-town little parties, and him making his way—no, not making, he disdained that trouble — he took it. His way he chose fitfully ; he selected anything at hazard, called it his way, and others cheerfully bowed and adopted it. There are a few such men in the world, and I have often envied them. Such a manner is worth money and place and estate. See how long one of us takes to carry out a little play, to get to know people, even. We hesitate, make timorous advances, lose days and weeks. He does all in a few minutes. Time, in this short life, is money, and more valuable. An ill-looking, wild-eyed man—cruel, I know— *that would kick a dog out of his way* instead of taking one step aside. This is a certain test of character and an acute one, which dear Mr. Barnard—and God bless him !—with all his knowledge of the world, and *my* ignorance of it, would never light on.

I dare say all this time he heartily disliked me—I am sure he did—and had that instinctive dislike which one man often has to another, from the very outset. His eyes seemed to challenge me, and he knew me for an adversary. How could I expect to compete with him, with such advantages on his side? And he had a great one, for in those days, my dear Dora, you were a little, ever so little, of a coquette, and liked to have your amusement, which was very natural indeed. "Flirt" I would not associate your dear name with. Odious and debasing word, which we will leave to the heartless professionals.

I had my trials. My father had speculated and lost a fine estate, which he had also encumbered. We had all then to work, and do what we could. Still, was I not a gentleman, and, though not a rich one, quite as good as they? But they looked down on me, because we had lost our fortune.

Grainger cast his eyes on her, just to fill up his idle time. For me he affected contempt, but from me he was to have a lesson. They wished to force her to marry him, and she was helpless in their hands. But when I heard that scandal about the innkeeper's daughter, where, too, he was lodging, was I not right to hunt it up? Could I have stood by and looked on? And though they said, and he protested, it was false, what of that? Did I not know him to be a man of a certain life? There were other stories about him as bad. He was not fit to be her husband, and if he did "go to the bad" later, it concerned himself, and merely proved my discernment. Dora's father had bitterly resented what she had done, and all her fortune and estate, too, was left away to a cousin—a drinking, hunting fellow—who was amazed at his good fortune. I never regretted it a moment. Shall I forget that scene, when Grainger was unmasked!—that morning when the proofs were given. He was afraid to lay a finger on me, but the look he gave! —the ferocious, evil look. He affected to despise me, to think me below his anger; but he little knew to what I was hurrying. He said, "Keep out of my way, for your own sake. It would not be worth my trouble to give myself the least exertion to punish you; but if ever I have a disengaged moment——" His look finished the rest. Insolent! *He* was unworthy my notice. The relatives were grateful. They did not suspect *then*. My family were Presbyterians, and they did not dream that one of that faith could ever presume.

Thank God I saved her! and I can now lay my hand on my heart and feel no compunction whatever. . . .

O that happy first year! She changed the whole colour of my life, made me thoughtful, steady, and taught me even to pray, which I did little of before. Angel! she shall teach me much more yet.

CHAPTER VI.

Saturday.—Homburg at last: delightful, and most easy journey. I have written my letter to her from this sweet and pastoral place. I write in the daintiest of little rooms, the yellow jalousies drawn close to keep out the sun. Outside the window is a balcony, Venetian-like in its breadth, filled up with a whole garden of flowers, where there is a table, and where one can actually walk about. It recals our old and lost place in the country, before we were ruined, as they say. Overhead is an awning, and when the sun is less strong, I can go out, and walk up and down, and look into the street. If only *she* were here! No matter; one of these days she shall be, and better times will come; "one colour cannot always be turning up," as the maid said this morning. And here comes in the post —a fellow like a soldier, with a very grim moustache, who hands in a letter. It is from her—I could guess at her writing from the very balcony. I run down to take it from the landlady's hands, and tear it open. I run up again as light and gay as ever I was in my life. It seems a whole year since I have seen her. Dear characters! sweet writing! I fasten it in here, at this page of my little diary.

"DEAREST,—Oh, how I miss and long for you. How I long to learn that you have borne the journey well; *not that you are better already, for that I am not so unreasonable as to expect.* But soon you will

tell me so. Our little darlings only know
that you have gone away. I suppose they
think it is only for a walk, to the nearest
town, and that you will be back. Don't
fatigue yourself writing, think only of your
dear health. Keep out of the dreadful
sun, and amuse yourself. I hope this will
find you on your arrival.

" DORA."

The underlined words, how delicate, how
like her sweet soul! She has a faint notion, but she dares not let it appear, that I
am a little better. I shall write this moment—what joyful news for her! . . . .
There, I have told her all, everything.
Four closely written pages and a *little*
swimming of the head; but I could almost
work at the ledger this moment.

I have told her how I was out betimes
this morning, at six o'clock; how I walked
up the bright street lined with fairy-look-

ing houses, all with their short broad balconies loaded with flowers. Then how I strolled past the gay festive pavilions more than hotels, the Four Seasons, the Victoria, with the cool shady courts and porches; past that turn to the right, down another sweet alley, where are more fairy-like houses with balconies, and where the great ones live. The Kisseleff-street they call it, which gives a grand and inspiring Russian association. All this time in front of me, as I ascend, and seemingly far away, yet very close, are the rich, cool, heavily laden Taunus hills, covered with trees and verdure, rising slowly and grandly, and filling up the gap between the houses at the far end of the town. Then I walk on upwards, and see the guests and strangers—the lovers of pleasure, in white coats and straw Panama hats, sitting out in front of the hotels, and smoking in the shade. Then I

4—2

pass the great red building, the Kursaal, which looks like a king's palace. I did not know *then* what it was, or what mysteries it held, yet there was a strange undefined awe came on me as I went by.

Then I turn down to the right, past the most inviting villas, all colours and shapes, now a Swiss châlet, now a true Italian house, but overgrown with the most exquisite foliage, the metal of their balconies all embroidered with leaves, behind which you see white dresses, and from behind which comes the clink of breakfast china. Then the houses stop short, and the dense greenery begins, groves upon groves, forest mounting over forest, walks winding here and winding there. Other windows, windows lower down, are thrown wide open, and there the morning meal goes on, even in the gardens; fat men in white coats and no waistcoats, with four double chins at least, are enjoying pipe and coffee. Along the path, honest Homburgers have their little table with an awning, under which is the cool melon, the grape, the delicious honey, and mountain butter, most inviting. If Dora were but on my arm how she would enjoy all this, as, indeed, I must stop in this description to tell her.

What an enchanting place! I never knew what "al fresco" meant before. The feeling of lightness and happiness on me I cannot describe; and I felt, too, that I was of them, and not a stranger, or country-town bred at all. Well, I walk on through this greenery, through the most charming alleys, cut in the groves, and, through the trees, see afar the glitter of company, the sheen of curious figures flitting to and fro among the leaves, the glimpse of a Swiss châlet. Such crowds—it seems like a Watteau feast! Down through the avenues

float the balmiest breezes, health restoring
as I feel when they touch me. Then I
emerge on the open space, and see the most
animated scene, bright colours, bright
dresses, white coats, grey coats, hats white
and grey, fluttering veils, pink and cream-
coloured parasols, flowers, "costumes" of
every pattern—all actually like the opening
scene of the chorus at an opera seen long,
long ago. From a pagoda come strains of
rich music, with the clash of cymbals and
soft stroke of drum. How new, how delicious all this to me! In the centre was
the well, deep below, with spacious steps
leading down, girls handing up the water,
and crowds pressing forward to receive it.
The clinking of glass everywhere. Beyond
again, rows of little shops for jewellery and
trifles—charming and most exhilarating
scene, as I look on. The animation and
gaiety drive away all the sinking and

weakness, and I seem to grow strong and hopeful every moment. Down the steps do they troop, the loveliest of women, French, English, and American, as I know by the curious chatter of the voices, and with them lords, and friends, and admirers of all kinds.

CHAPTER VII.

THE Briton—of course I knew him by his talking so loud about "my breakfast." How often do I hear that florid, white-whiskered father, suffering from the heat acutely, tell his friend and tell me—for he does not care who hears him, and prefers an audience—that "he'd speak to Gungl, at the Hesse, about giving us some more of that wild deer," or "that he was going to get his cutlets, and very odd the *Times* was so late;" or else, what seems the standard grumble, about "kreutzers" and "their infernal money. Look here, I say, what can you make of such things as these?" He actually does seem to think, that wherever the Englishman goes, the Englishman's money, meats, steaks, joints, beds, clubs, *Times*, &c., should go with him, and be the money, meat, steaks of the country. My dearest Dora, will you know me after this, or do you suppose it is your poor invalid that is writing? Such a change in me already—affecting to be funny! Indeed, I think I could write an amusing book of travels, and perhaps I shall, one of these days. Acute observation is perhaps all that is wanted.

But I go on. Then I see the great doctor of the place, Seidler, whose book, "Homburg and its Springs," is in every bookseller's window. He is walking about here, talking to the English, who hang on his very words, and his carriage and horses wait at the end of the walk—a good advertisement, for every stranger asks whose it is. My old friend the Briton with the white whiskers, I remark, is great on Seidler. At dinner he tells every one what "Seidler said to me this morning. Seidler made me cut off a tumbler of the kayser-browning, and told me if I had taken it another day he would not have answered for it. Egad! I was working away hard, and if he hadn't stopped me," &c. Seidler, I can see, is looked on as a magician who can do as he likes with the springs, and mysteriously check their whole efficiency if you offend him. Any one who takes them without consulting *him* goes to destruction at once; or else they do the patient no good at all. We might all be as well quaffing common spring water. A third of a tumbler, he will say, every half-hour in the morning, or a tumbler at seven, and half a tumbler at *a quarter to ten*. The idea seems to be that, delayed till *ten*, the pre-

scription would have no efficacy; or that
an eighth more in quantity would be fatal;
and I see the fresh white-whiskered man,
watch in hand, counting the moments.
Of course I went myself to Seidler, and
believe him to be clever; and he certainly
hit off my case at once. But these little
tricks the English themselves force on him,
as their maladies are so tricky and fanciful.
He says that three weeks of the water, and
of Seidler—three tumblers of the former,
and one interview with the latter per diem
—"will make a new man of me." And I
do believe him. I am a new man already.
My dear, shall I confess it, I can now bear
this separation, and am *not* craving to be
back. It will be better in the end I should
be here. But after ten days I know I
shall get restless, and eager to see your
pretty face. Now, dear, I stop this log, for
I have to go to the baths. To-morrow I

go into Frankfort on the business, having
heard from the merchant, who has fixed an
hour to see me. He talks of some difficulty, but I shall work hard, and do everything to show our gratitude to our dear benefactor. And if I can conclude the matter
on more favourable terms, and save him
some money, shall I not lessen my obligation a little? I find a gentleman whom I
met in the walks, and who seems to have a
sort of interest in me, is going back to
London to-night. I shall send him what I
have written so far, and he will post it in
London to Dora.

CHAPTER VIII.

Saturday.—The first portion of the log has gone off. She will have it by Monday, and I know it will amuse them all.

At twelve to-day, I again pass by the grand red granite building, of a rich handsome stone, and which *is* indeed Homburg. It is in the centre of the town, in the street, but has a garden in front; with a row of orange trees, considered the noblest in the world. There is really something grand in the air of these magnificent strangers, each in his vast green box, and standing, I suppose, thirty feet high. The greatest and most tender care is taken of them: men are always watering, washing, cleaning, coifféing these aristocrats, morning, noon, and night. They are allowed to appear abroad during the hot months only, and when the cooler period sets in, they are tenderly moved to a vast palace far off in the woods, built expressly for them, where they live toge-ther all the winter, with fires, and blanket-ing, and matting, and everything luxu-rious. The story runs that they were all lost, one by one, by a certain landgrave, or elector, or grand duke, who staked them against some hundred pounds apiece; and now this brings me to what I have been indirectly fencing off, and which fills me with a certain dread, as I think of it.

I never felt such a sensation, as when, after passing through the noble passage floored with marble, three or four hundred feet long, where a whole town might pro-menade, I found myself in a vast cool,

shaded hall, that seemed like the ban-
queting-room of a palace. It was of noble
proportions, carved ceiling, and literally
one mass of gorgeous fresco-painting and
gold. Glittering chandeliers of the most
elegant design hang down the middle, the
arches in the ceiling are animated with
figures of nymphs and cupids, with gardens
and terraces, and porticos, while the fur-
nishing is rich, solid, and in the most exquisite taste. From these open other rooms,
seen through arches and the folds of lace
curtains beyond, and each decorated in a
different taste—one, snowy white and gold,
another, pale pink and gold. The floors
are parquet, in the prettiest patterns.
Servants in rich green and gold liveries
glide about, and there are most luxurious
soft couches in crimson velvet, lining the
walls. What art has done is indeed all
perfect and most innocent; but where na-

ture and humanity gathers round, standing in two long groups down the room, another *hand* has been at work. It almost appals. For now, for the first time, I hear the music, the faint, prolonged " a-a-a-rr." Then comes the clatter, and sudden rattle and chinking of silver on silver, of gold on gold, and the low short sentences of those who preside over the rite, and—silence again. As I join the group and look over shoulders, then I see that strange human amphitheatre, that oval of eager and yet impassive faces, all looking down on the bright green field—of the cloth of gold, indeed.

What a sight! the four magicians, with their sceptres raised—the piles of gold, the rouleaux, the rich coils of dollars like glittering silver snakes, and more dangerous than any snake—the fluttering notes nestling in little velvet-lined recesses, and peeping out through the gilt bars of their little cages. There is something awful in this spectacle, and yet there is a silent fascination—something, I suppose, that must be akin to the spectacle at an execution.

Then the preparation, the prompt covering of the green ground in those fatal divisions, the notes here, the glittering pile of yellow pieces there, the solid handsome dollars whose clinking seems music, the lighter florins, the double-Fredericks, and the fat sausage-like rouleaux, which these wonderful and dexterous rakes adjust so delicately! Now the cards are being dealt slowly, while the most perfect stillness reigns, and every eye is bent on those hands. I hear the dealer, at the end of the first row, give a sort of grunt, with an "ung!"—then begin his second, and end with judgment or verdict. There is a general rustle and turning away of faces, a stooping forward, a marking of paper, while lo! the four fatal rakes begin sweeping in greedily gold and notes and silver—all in confusion, a perfect torrent — while, this fatal work over, two skilful hands begin to spout money, as it were, to the ends of the earth. On the fortunate heaps left undisturbed come pouring down whole Danae showers of silver and gold; and to the rouleaux come rolling over softly companion rouleaux. Now do eager fingers stretch out and clutch their prize: while faces, yellow and contorted, their fingers to their lips, look on dismally.

Then it begins again, figures stooping forward to lay on; and so the wretched formula goes on, repeated—for I made the calculation—some seven hundred times that day. But it never seems to flag, and every time has the air of fresh and fresher novelty. It begins to sicken me, and that air of stern concentrated attention, of sacrifice even, depresses me; and when I think that, if a return could be got of the agitation, palpitations, hopes, fears, despair, exultation, going on during these seven hundred operations, it would represent a total of human agony inconceivable. I see how it can be again multiplied through the twelve months of this wicked year. Then I think of the prospective miseries to others at a distance, to wives and to children—lives wretched, lives unsettled—miserable deaths. I say, I think of all this, and ask, Is it too much to call these men special ministers of Mephistopheles—a band under the decent respectable name of a Bank, organized to destroy souls by machinery, the like of which for completeness exists not in this world? I repeat, there is nothing on earth approaching this company, whose men and emissaries ought to wear cock's feathers and red and black dresses, for their complete and suc-

5—2

cessful exertions for destruction and corruption. They distil their poison over that green board, and it is carried away to all countries—to England, France, America, Belgium, Germany, whence the victims return again and again, bringing fresh ones, like true decoys. They hang men, they punish and imprison for far less crimes; but on the heads of these wretches is the ruin of thousands of bodies and souls, the spiritual death, and the actual *corporeal death* of thousands more, who have hung themselves to the fair trees planted in sweet bowers by the "administration," or stifled themselves with charcoal in front of this fatal palace, or who have actually dabbled over with their brains the vile green table on which they have lost all. A banking company! all fair, give and take, and such phrases! Satan says the same in *his* dealings.

And here is this functionary in the trim

suit—a pink-faced, hard, cat-eyed sinner, who steals about, and watches everybody, and his own agents also, more than any one else. A capital officer, they tell me, skilful and wary at the accounts. To him the shareholders will one day present a piece of plate, or hard cash, which he would prefer, in acknowledgment of his exertions in their interest. O that some fitting punishment could be devised for those who thus fatten on the blood of the innocent! Surely I should not come here. I should not breathe this tainted air—look on this painted vice, and their wretched shabby baits to win the approbation of the decent and the moral like myself. Here are our English news-papers of every kind and degree. Pray, they say, read all day long in these charm-ing rooms, and sit on these soft couches, or out here in these charming gardens while our music plays for you. *Do* understand, nothing is expected from you in return. You, charming English ladies, so fair and pretty, you can work here with those innocent fingers; and your nice, high-spirited brothers, they would like to get up cricket, would they not? Well here is a nice field; we shall have it mowed and got ready, and to-morrow shall come from Frankfort the finest bats, stumps, balls—everything complete. Do you give the order; or get them from London, if you like. We shall pay. There is shooting, too—quite of the best. We shall be proud to find the guns and dogs, and even the powder. It will do us an honour. Get up a little fête; a dance in the Salons des Princes. We shall light it up for you, and find the servants.

So do these tricksters try to impose on us, with their sham presents, but for which our Toms and Charleses—good-natured elder brothers—must pay, and pay secretly,

in many a visit to this table. They have
built us a superb theatre—one of the handsomest of its size in Europe. How kind,
how considerate! yet they charge us a napoleon for a stall, if there is any one worth
hearing. Presents, indeed! we know the
poor relative who comes with a twopenny-
halfpenny pot of jam, and expects to get a
handsome testimonial in return. Everything about our "administration" is in
keeping; and I almost grieve that I should
have come to such a place. This resolution,
at least, I can make: *never to let the light of
an honest man's face beam on their evil
doings.* What will they care? but it shall
be my protest.

I feel I am rather warm on this matter,
but it does seem to me that the whole has
been far too gently dealt with hitherto, and
treated too indulgently. Even these Prussian conquerors, who, we are told, have

given them notice that they are to be *chasséd*,
have shown too much respect. They talk
of equities and of a lease. Do we hold to
leases with pirates? Do we make treaties
with Bill Sikes? Had I been the king, I
would have marched two regiments into
their glittering halls, seized their infamous
tools, broken the rakes across the soldiers'
knees, torn up their cards, smashed into
firewood the roulette board and its num-
bers, impounded their gold and silver and
sent it off to the hospitals, and, locking the
doors and leaving sentries, have marched off
M. A—— and M. B——, their admirable
men of business, in a file of soldiers. I
should have these fellows tried, and put to
hard labour for the rest of their lives. As
it is, a culpable weakness has given them
three or four years more to pursue their
vile work, and gather, say, twenty thousand
precious souls into Satan's own bag-net!

CHAPTER IX.

Eleven o'clock at Night.—I really cannot endure this terrible spectacle any more, and shall not go to that place again. What I have seen to-night is almost awful. I went into those rooms, now lit up, rich in colours, and glittering like a king's palace. Such a crowd, and such a contrast! First, I had gone on the terrace, and looked down on the charming gardens, where the innocent were at the little tables, each surrounded with its group, sipping coffee; the music playing in the pavilion. Then I turn round and look at the blazing windows, at the great door behind me, which yawns like a cavern.

I hear the faint " click-click" and " rattle-rattle," and that vast and quiet group crowded together.   They were serious and earnest; but there are delighted and festive groups, wandering about—happy families, charming young girls, good-natured papas and mammas looking on with delight.   And now one of the young girls comes tripping back with " Charles," in *such* delight, showing something shining in her hand.   The great soft couches round are lined with festive-looking people.   Every one is " circulating," and there is an air of animation and motion over all.   Some curiosity makes me linger, and share it also—a wish to describe to my little darling at home such a strange and singular phase of manners and character.

I draw near to that other table—the one I had not watched in the morning, and which is consecrated to roulette.   It glitters

all over with pieces, sown thickly, sown
broadcast, dotted here, there, and everywhere, in perfect spasms of distribution.
They contend with each other, this yellow,
fiery-eyed, and dirty man, and the keen but
pretty girl with powder an inch thick on
her face, and her pink silk gathered up about
her. They grudge each other room, do
these combatants; they glare savagely; the
old lady in black silk guides, with a trembling hand, her single piece to some number
dimly seen, but whose place she guesses at.
As the ball flies round in its tiny circus,
every arm, with long-stretched wrist, lunges
out, eager to be on; piece jostles piece.
"Give us standing room," they say, no matter
whether they have lost or won. Then comes
the sudden leap and metallic click, as the ball
stumbles into its bed ; then the waterfall
comes spouting down from the centre—the
heavy streams of coin, directed and lighting

with pleasant jingling on its fellows. No
one seems daunted by defeat. I see one
man who has been frantically piling his gold
here, there, and everywhere, and, by some
strange and *devilish* perversity, is not allowed
to win—no, not once—while little, mean,
cautious fiddling folk, with their florins and
francs, fare admirably. I see him biting
his lips as his nervous fingers turn over the
half-dozen little gold pieces, in that agoniz-
ing uncertainty which I note so often,
whether to play the bold game now, risk
all, or save this little wreck for another
season. And all to be decided within a
second! When it is gone, a pause, and then
that rueful *walking away* off the stage, while
others rush into his place.

Or the case of another. His all seems
gone; when, after an undecided council, his
hand seeks his breast-pocket—a note to be
changed—something that he has no right to

meddle with! Then the girls, young, pretty, and not innocent of fear; then the ladies— good sensible wives at home, but trans- formed by coming to these places—gradually becoming greedy harpies, and ready, if they lose, to turn, cat-like, on their husbands. Ah! there is the true demon's work—not the mere loss of money. All this wreck, this shocking wreck, caused by this factory of wickedness!

I have had enough for one day and for one night. I wish I had not seen it, for it makes me wretched; and yet it is worth seeing as a spectacle of infamy. What I have written, too, will interest my pet at home; and, as I know she hoards up every scrap of my writing, perhaps one day others will find it, and read it, and it may act as a warning. There! I am going to bed infi- nitely better. God be praised for his mercy! and for my pet's sake I will say over

her little prayer, which she, I know, will be
saying about the same time:

*" O Lord! Thou who dost guide the ship
over the waters, and bring safe to its journey's
end the fiery train, look on me in this distant
land.   Save me from harm of soul and body;
give me back health and strength, that I may
serve Thee more faithfully, and be able to bring
others dependent on me to serve Thee also,
and add to Thy glories!   Amen."*

Sunday.—How sweet and delicious are
the mornings here; what soft airs blow
gently from these luxuriant trees and mountains!   One really grows fonder of the
place every moment.   These mornings are
the most charming; ever so pastoral, and
yet it will seem but the pastoral air of the
theatre or the opera—sham trees and shep-
herdesses; and I feel all the time that the
corrupting Upas spreads its fatal vanities
over all.   These pretty wells, enchanting

walks, innocent flowers, music, lights, trees, ferns, what not—they could hardly exist without *this* support. The odious and plundering vice keeps up and pays for all, even for the innocent blessings of nature; and I *do* doubt whether one is not accessory before the act to those results, in accepting *any* benefit from so contaminated a source, and lending *one's countenance* in return to their doings. But this is too much refining, and my pet at home will smile at such scruples. I must not set up to be a saint, and I shall do more practical work if, by word or example, I can save some light and careless soul from the temptation. Some way I seem to myself to be grown a little too virtuous since I came here; but in presence of this awful destroyer it is hard not to be serious.

A great bait to purchase the good will of the decent is the reading room, flooded

literally with journals of all climes. Squire
John Bull is paid special attention to, by
half a dozen—his favourite *Times*, *Pall Mall*,
Morning Herald even—though what put
that journal in the heads of the administration it would be hard to tell—and the
veteran Galignani. Only a glass door between the *Times* and the squire, who is
stingy at heart, and resents postage, and at
the same time having to subscribe to his
club at home, where he can have all these
papers for nothing—British flesh and blood
cannot stand *that;* so he and his wife—I
know him at once by his gold glass and
complacent air as he reads—come every
morning at eleven o'clock, and sit and de-
vour their cheap news till one or two. The
greediness and selfishness displayed as to
getting papers by these people is inconceivable. I do say there is more of the little
mean vices engendered in that room than

one could possibly conceive in so small a space. The moment he enters, there is the questing eye looking round with suspicion and eagerness until he sees the mainsail of his *Times* fluttering in another Briton's hand—an old enemy—i.e. one who is a slow reader, and who reads every word. He himself is a slow reader, and reads every word; but *that* is nothing to the point. A look of dislike and anger spreads over his face: but there is the other copy, also "in hand"—in the hand of a dowager, with glasses also—"that *beast* of a woman," he tells his wife. The person in whose hands he likes to see his *Times* is a young thing, a "chit of a girl," who just skims over a column or two, reads the *Court Circular* portion, and the account of the latest opera. Though indeed, he thinks that she has no business to be reading at all. He prowls about, looking at the owners of other papers,

as who should say. "Ugh, you!" Now
some one lays down a paper, and he rushes
at it, anticipating another cormorant by a
second: it is only the *old* journal, not
yesterday's.   Then, with eyes of discontent,
he goes up to the reader in possession of
the *Times*, and says, bitterly, "I'll trouble
you, when you have done with *that;*" to
which the answer is a grunt.   And then he
draws a chair close opposite to that reader,
and if glaring can hurry, or restless moving
of the chair, or impatient ejaculation, he
cannot fail.   When he *does* secure it,
what a read he has, and how he does take
it out of the others!   If he could he would
have three or four—one to sit on, one lying
near him, another under his arm or behind
his back.   And yet he is not a bad man, I
am sure, at home; but the very atmosphere
of this place, perverts everything.   The
French and Germans in this room take the

thing more tranquilly. They read their little newspaper quietly and swiftly, with a little faint eagerness to get possession of the *Figaro*, or some diverting paper; but no one glares at his neighbour. My Dora at home will send me out a paper, so I shall be independent of these rascals and their pitiful bribes.

Two o'clock.—The dogs in the street drawing the little milk carts, harnessed so neatly, and drawing so willingly, are a pretty sight. Honest Tray, with his broad jaws well open, and he himself panting from the heat, looks up every now and again to the neat German girl who walks by him. When she wants him to go on she leads him gently by his great yellow ear, as if it was a bridle. When there are two together, they trot on merrily; but the work is too much for the poor paws of a single fellow. When they are waiting, I

6—2

notice she draws them into the shade, and they lie down there, in their harness.

I must tell you, dearest, about the people here, for this is a great place in which to study human nature and character. All the tribes of the earth seem to come here, and take a new sort of shape as they stay. It is a paradise for women, and for pretty women, and therefore if my pet were here, —but I must not turn that pretty head which the London sculptor wished to model. Neither should I like her to be exposed to the bold, free-and-easy study of some of the gentry who walk about here, and survey beauty leisurely. In England, did any venture to "stare," as we would call it, in such a fashion, we should be tempted to fetch him a good stroke across his insolent face. But here, in this gathering of all the licentious free lances of Europe, it is tolerated and *invited* even. Yes,

women are actually proud of this question-
able sort of attention, and they give a look
in return, though only a second's length, as
if to challenge fresh attention. And yet it
must be owned, our own decent, decorous
dames and girls, do look a poor race here;
they seem to want style, which is with
beauty colour, everything save expression.
There is, indeed, a charming-looking girl,
who walks about here with a sister, and has
an air of enjoyment and delight truly refreshing in the *fade* indifference which
prevails. She has the most mysterious
likeness to my Dora at home: I am glad
she is here, as she will be a little photo-
graph of one who is so dear to me. The
same expression, the same aristocratic look
that *she* has. Petite, with an exquisitely-
shaped head, the richest and glossiest dark
hair, the most refined outline of face; I am
struck with her more and more.

What contrasts to her the Americans, dressed to extravagance in theatrical " costumes," as they call laces and flounces, and the shortest of dresses, the highest of heels, some certainly two or three inches high! Their faces are surprisingly round and full and brilliant, their figures good and handsome, which is a surprise; but when they open their full lips out streams the twang, nasal and horny. I shall see more of them, however, at a ball to be given presently.

I know some little details of their dress, &c., will amuse my pet. What will she say to a rich black silk Watteau dress, looped and curtained up, all over embroidery, with a crimson Spanish petticoat seen below, the black all lit up here and there with the most delicate little lines and edging of crimson? It is as delicate as a Cardinal's undress. " What will I say," I hear my pet answer, "simply this—It would cost half a year's salary." Then what will she say to a faint amber-coloured summer dress, all looped and hanging in festoons, with a pale blue and white petticoat? This is indeed dressing in water colour, and both belong to an American. There is another, a sort of pale sprite of a fairy, so white and delicate are her cheeks, so lustrous her eyes, so artificial the effect. She is all eternal smiles and giggling, and writhing and twisting of the neck, a favourite part of American pantomime. Her dress is becomingly short, abolishing the oft-quoted Sir John Suckling's line; for here ladies feet do not, like little mice, "run in and out," but rather arrogantly display themselves, peacock-like, as ostentatiously as they can. We might find patterns here of the plumage of all the birds of the air, from the flamingo downward; with a good deal of damaged ware, which I would not for the world my pet saw, but this is only more of the work of the Mephistopheles company yonder. To think, again, I say, that these pure blessings, these life-giving springs, sent to give strength and innocence, all to be turned into fresh agents for attracting villany and vice. Was there ever such diabolical perversity!

There is an American family sitting opposite, at table d'hôte, whom I shall just touch off. The men are odious, and the whole family deceptive. I sit next them the first day, and think they are intelligent, and rational, and moderate, and that we have done the country some injustice. There is a father with a coal-black wig and walnut face next to me; an elderly and simpering wife, with another wig, next to him; opposite are young and rising Americans—two youths and a girl. The walnut face enters readily into conversation, that is, makes statements in an odd sort of way, rolling his eyes with an accompanying grin after each statement, and going into gastronomic raptures; not only that, but, according to the slang phrase, "going into" the delicacies themselves without fear or restraint. Even into the salad, though the doctor has warned him. This meal is the paradise of red-faced old men, who do indeed gorge themselves, and think they can repair all disasters by a morning's walk and a few tumblers at the spring.

A question to my neighbour reveals the Yankee by an interrogative reply: "Seeyer?" as who should say, "What d'ye say to that, stranger?" As, for instance, "I were secretary o' state for Lueczana in the yeer '20;" interrogative and sudden goggling of the eyes. I bow, and say, "Indeed!" "Oh, but, yes I we-ere. In the year '25, ser, the

President he sent for me, and consul-ted
me on the then money crisis, he did."
Grin of delight and rolling of the eyes. " I
were at *your* court, ser, in the year '30, on
a special mission to our min'ster, I wee-ere."
After these little preliminaries he grows a
little interesting about some recollections
of the older American gentlemen, and I
begin to think him an intelligent and sensible, though odd American. But the next
day a harmless observation of mine as to
the inconvenience resulting to the public
departments from all employés going out
with the President, caused a complete
change. The cloven hoof was put down on
the table. The little European plating
came off. I had scraped the Russian and
found the snob. " Yew," he said, "yew
had no police in yewer city before the yeer
'40. The streets of London were unsafe to
walk in. Yewer State, sir, is decaying

fast. We're coming up fast, rapidly; yewer goin' down."

On this tack the whole family opened. One said, apropos of nothing, that "yewer kynage was all debased. The gold weren't pure, and the selver bad." The lady added, very nasally, that what annoyed her was the English saying that the Americans talked through their noses. "Now, I'm shewer, yewer cockneys, and yewer Yorkshire, and yewer Irish and Scotch, they do talk queer." On this, the discussion got a little inflamed, and rather personal on both sides.

You may tell our dear Mr. Barnard, that no one has yet found out that I come from a country town. They think I lived all my life in Town.

CHAPTER X.

Monday.—I am not sorry that I adopted that resolution of forswearing the Kursaal and its reading-rooms, though I *did* see Mr. Lewis, the clergyman of the English chapel, going in and sitting down, and reading his Galignani. Can he really know what he is doing? He is on the spot, a resident, and it is, as it were, in his parish. Well, at all events, it is his concern. I even saw him enter from the colonnade, go up the steps into the great cavern entrance and pass through. He was, I suppose, looking for some one. Still, if I were to refine on the matter, this garden where

I am now, is theirs, kept by their gar-
deners. This very seat on which I sit, was
paid for by them. Now what do you say,
Dora? Send me some little bit of casuistry
to help me over the matter. . . . .

What scenes I do see, even so far off as
I am now; hints, as it were, of a whole
history. Thus have I come in late to a
theatre, and, standing in the box lobby,
have peeped in, through the little glass
window in the door. That glimpse has a
strange mystery, from the fact of all having
been worked up to a point, abrupt to
you. The situation seems overcharged, we
who look are in quite another region—a
long way behind, as it were. I have noticed a fair-haired youth with a gold
" pinch-nose," and who is certainly not
more than twenty, and on his arm is a
charming little French girl of seventeen,
round and rosy, and dressed in the most

piquant way imaginable. I soon found out that they are just married, not further back than a month. They were supremely happy, like children, running from one thing to another, and enjoying everything with a surprising happiness and animation. He wore a straw-coloured silk coat and white hat—she, a most coquettish little hat and a pink and white short dress.

On the first day I had noticed them standing at the mouth of what I call " the yawning cave," hesitating gently, she looking in with the strangest air of curiosity, half in amazement, half in awe. Then I see them go in, and really that seemed, by a sort of instinct, to be for me the beginning of something that would end tragically. Their look of supreme happiness seemed, I suppose, to imply a contrast and supplement of disaster. In half an hour I saw them come back, she triumphant, fluttering, he with a complacent and boyish smile, looking at something bright in his hand. She skipped and danced and clapped her hands. I might suppose they had won. They were children, and I had a surprising interest in them—I know not why. . . . .

I dined to-day at the Four Seasons Hotel, which at these places is always said to be a most gay and festive-looking hotel, with orange trees in front, and a kind of scene-painting air. So an old gentleman, who had been all round the watering-places, told me. He could not account for it, he said, but there it was. I accounted for it to him by the invincible power of names. Give a girl, I said, a pretty and romantic name, like Geraldine, or Dorcas, or Violet, and she will be sure in some degree to fall into the *key* of that pretty music. *He* did not seem to see it, but grunted and moved away from me. An-

other man said, "he supposed it paid,"—a
coarse view, which did not touch the
matter. These table d'hôtes are certainly
the most festive way of eating a dinner.
There is such variety in the faces, such
pretty, intellectual, or stupid, heavy faces
—faces, indeed, that seem to have been
turned all day long towards that dinner,
and wistfully expecting it. A long narrow
room, yet so bright and airy, and looking
on the street; I can fancy nothing so
cheerful. Every one is in good humour;
and even the waiters have a festive air,
principally, I believe, from their being boys
and boyish, as is the custom here, and not
the mouldy, ancient, clumsy-legged, clumsy-
fingered veterans who do duty with us.
And what a good dinner—what a choice of
wine, instead of our limited sherry, and
claret, and " Bass." The little flasks dot
the table down. Their Affenthaler, ordi-

nary, but good; the yellow hocks, infinite in variety; the better Assmanshausen, and the hockheimer sparkling, all at *such* moderate prices. I see *complete* families pour in, and take up position in line, father, stout mother, pleasant daughters, and the conceited son. Then the dinner sets in like a torrent; all the pleasant German dishes; those vegetables which we know not of in England, and best of all, those delicious fowls, wherewith arrives the late but welcome salad. It does seem to me that it comes at the precise and fitting moment, with a pleasant sense of expectancy going before it, he and his friend the fowl. My dear Dora will hardly think that this can be her old invalid that is speaking.

On this day I find myself seated next to the little husband and wife of the morning, who come in full of delight and satisfaction, and smiling they know not why. I con-

fess I am glad to be near so much innocence, and also on account of a little scheme
I have in view. With such a pair, it is
not difficult to begin a conversation. They
were glad of the sympathy. My dear Dora
knows that my stock of French is tolerably
respectable, and that I can put it to fair
use. They spoke together, and told me
everything about themselves. They were
not rich, but had enough. They were
enjoying themselves so. It was the most
delicious place in the world. " It was
heaven itself," she said; "and do you
know," she added, " all the money we made
—that is, he made—to-day, and so easily—
eight napoleons; and out of it he bought
me this sweet little ˙brooch." And she
showed on her breast what was certainly a
very charming little ornament. This
naïveté and her agreeable prattle began to
interest me a great deal; but I could see

there was in *him* a certain boyish self-sufficiency—a latent idea that this *gaming success was chiefly owing to his own cleverness.* He talked very wisely about the principles. I quietly ventured to hint that luck might change, as it did so often and so fatally. But he only laughed. Just as dinner was nearly over, a friend sent in to him; he went out, and I was left with the charming little wife. Something inspired me to seize the opportunity, and give a little warning to this interesting young creature.

"Your husband," I said, "seems quite excited about his success; but may I give you a piece of advice? The beginning ends always in the same way. You know not how fatal is this spell, once it gets any influence. The rage for play, if it takes possession of any one, destroys all—*love, happiness,* everything else. I know it, and every one here knows it."

7—2

This way of putting it was a little artful, and I saw it had great effect. The pretty face looked a little scared. I went on.

" I speak sincerely and in your interest, though I am a mere stranger; and I *do* advise you and warn you, to take care and not encourage your husband in this pursuit. There is no harm done as yet, and be content with your little spoils." This may seem a little too indulgent, too complacent, to the evil practice, against which I have sworn war to the knife, to the death, and from which, with the blessing of Heaven, I shall rescue many. But such a foe it is pardonable to meet with craft like his own.

He then came back, but I saw she had grown thoughtful. It was something to do a little bit of good, even in this cheap way. I see them at night, hovering about the yawning entrance to the cave, she, with a little hesitation whispering him earnestly, and looking in with trepidation. They do not see me. They walk away, but alas, come back and enter.

Still the seed is sown. It may have done good. It is really amazing this instinct I have of all the working of this infamous system. I might have been a veteran gambler; though *their* knowledge is not much.

CHAPTER XI.

Tuesday.—But I must leave these minor things quite out of sight, to come to the strangest thing that has ever happened, one of the most mysterious and inconceivable. Could I ever have dreamt of it? And yet I am not sorry. Dora, dearest, prepared for something dramatic!

Let me begin calmly. Last night, after the young pair had gone in, I was sitting under the long glass colonnade of the terrace, looking down on the crowd in those gardens, lit up by the twinkling lamps, and which have such a charm for me. Along that colonnade are about a hundred little tables, all crowded with eager and lively people, sipping drinks, taking iced beer, champagne—happy winners, and more dismal losers. The waiters are flying up and down, hurrying to and fro, shouting orders; while below, among the green trees and flowers, are the crowds seated, and on the right the illuminated kiosque, with the delicious Prussian band pouring out their strains. "Ravishing" is but a poor word for these accomplished musicians, who belong to the Thirty-fourth Regiment, and are led by the skilful "chapel-master," Parlow. Their vast strength and breadth of sound, their rich instruments, with every instrument made the most of, their exquisite taste, volume, clearness, distinctness, and mastery of the most difficult passages, makes their performance almost entrancing. Hear them play three overtures—William Tell, Tännhauser, and Oberon—and the musician will be amazed as well as enraptured, the marvellous violin passages of the last being performed like so much child's-play—just as an accomplished pianoforte player runs up and down the keys. Hear them, too, in some fantasia on airs from L'Africaine or Faust, and revel in the taste and feeling of the solos, and the dramatic bursts and crashes, and the "hurrying" and lingering of the time, as though they were an opera orchestra. When we think of our creatures —those groups of hodmen and mechanics who form what is by courtesy termed " a military band," those mere grinders and sawyers of music, who play as though they would dig or hammer—when we think, I say, of our "crack" regiments, our Guards, formed out of the very pink of professionals, and see how mediocre is the result, one must feel a little humiliation and some envy, and should be glad to come this distance and hear these Prussians. I can hear them, too, with a safe conscience, for *they* do not belong to my enemies the administration.

But I am putting off this wonderful surprise. Well, I was sitting there, listening, close also to the mouth of the cave, which has still for me that sense of mystery, when I hear some angry voices, and two men are coming down the steps in excitement. One is tall, and in a white Panama hat, and very excited. I hear him say, " It is always the way when I listen to your infernal talk. I'd have had a hundred in my hand now but for you. I could pitch you down these steps, on your face! Go away, I tell you— leave me alone !"

The voice seemed familiar to me—so cold and grating, with all its excitement, that I seemed to recal it perfectly. Unconsciously I started up to be quite certain, and, on the noise, he turned and looked at me. He knew me; I knew him.

His face turned livid, and a spasm of fury passed over it.

" Grainger !"

" Austen !"

He advanced towards me, and for a moment I thought he meant some violence. But he suddenly checked himself, and then walked away, down the terrace. Then, as suddenly turned back, and came up to me.

After a pause, he spoke. " So *you* are here.   Did you know that I was here?"

"No, Grainger," I answered, " I did not."

" What, no new scheme on hand?   No, I should say not; for you had better wait, *my friend*, until you know whether the old account has been closed."

" The only scheme I have," I answered, " is to get back some health, and life even, which is nearly gone from me."

" Ay. But do you know all that has gone from me—*all that you took from me?* Eh?—*all that you stole from me!* What do you say? Answer!"

Again there was something so threatening in his manner, that I half moved back, as if to defend myself.

"Oh, don't be afraid," he said; "we dare not do these things in this place. Here, kellner, come here, will you! Bring some red wine here, strong and good, and don't be an hour, with your ' V'la monsieur,' and all that humbug. Come, sit down, Mr. Austen; you may as well; I am not going to be violent, so you needn't be afraid. I want to let you know something which you ought to know."

" Grainger," I said, "when all that took place, you had your opportunity. I met you fairly and——"

" *Met me fairly!*" he repeated, his eyes

dropping on me with a flash, " can you say that—you who set up to be a moral and praying man!" Then he laughed. "But, my good friend, that is all so long ago. An old story like that must not be exhumed. Let it rot away in the ground. Dead leaves— nothing but a pile of decayed dead leaves! If you don't rake them up, I promise you I shall not. There. Come! let us have something, as earnest. You shall pay for me, who was the loser then, and I *think* the injured man."

Something in this phrase struck me, and I felt there was some truth in what he said. He was the defeated party; I was the victor, and ought to be generous.

"What shall it be," I said, " champagne?"

" Do you take me for an American?" he said, with a laugh. " No, cognac. Now let us talk. I have forgiven and forgotten all that—though it ruined me for ever and ever, amen. I had a sort of infatuation over me. She, that girl—I mean Mrs. Austen, made me a miserable fool. If she had come here, I would have followed her. I'd have played my body and soul, that is, if I had seen a chance. But you had it all your own way. How does she look now—does she hate me? Come, tell me! And yet a good deal is on her gentle head. This is my life now, poor me; a 'hell,' to many others. You saw what I was then, a gentleman, at least well off, respected—own that! Well, I had to leave the army; I did something I ought not to have done, from sheer desperation. Yes, I did, and sank lower and lower, and all this was your joint work; but I don't want to blame you. By Jove, it is I who am raking up the dead leaves after all! Ah, here's the cognac."

I felt a pity for him. There was truth

in what he said. Since you, Dora, had been saved from him, all these troubles had come upon him. He had grown desperate; he was at least privileged to speak as he pleased, and have that slight consolation. I saw, too, that he was altered. At *that* time he was considered by the women a good-looking man, his face having a little of that rude gauntness which is not un-pleasing. He had large eyes, and a black irregular beard and moustache. Now he had grown careless in his dress. I knew how much that portended, and felt a deep pity for him.

"Grainger," I said, "it was hard for you, for I know you loved her. But I declare solemnly here, that my loving her had nothing to do with it, and you know your-self, Grainger, a marriage with you could not have been for her happiness, after that business——"

His brow contracted, his eye glared. "I know what you mean," he said. "That was false, false as hell False as I sit here, and hope to be——Well, I have much hope of *that*."

"They *said* it was true," I said; "but even to have such a rumour, and in the case of a fair innocent young girl——Admit yourself, Grainger, it could not be."

He answered in a low voice, "It was all false—a lie, an invention. There was the sting. Of course I cannot prove it; but suppose it untrue, what punishment would you say was enough for the one who did me so horrid an injury? Would a whole life be too long to devote to punishing the doer of such an injury?"

"You cannot mean me?" I said.

"Well, I *did* mean you *then*," he said. "I suppose, if there had been opportunity, I could have killed you. But that is all

over, all past and gone. Nothing could
make Roly Poly as he was before. The
eggshell is broken, and the yolk run out.
So tell me about yourself, and about her.
What brings you here?"

There was something so frank, so generous, so valorous, in this way of taking the
thing, that with an involuntary motion I
put out my hand and grasped his. Shall I
say, too, I felt a sudden twinge of conscience; and had all along a dim foreboding
that the story might not have been true,
or at least, have got its colouring of truth
from what might have been interested
motives on my side? I was too much concerned, perhaps, to be impartial, and if he
was innocent, then some share in this work
might be laid to my account. What was
plainly my duty, was to try and compensate
in some way, at least by kindness—for I
had not much else at my command—for so

cruel a wrong as this. I complied heartily with his wish; told him all that brought me here, and the business I was about. He listened attentively. Then we wandered back, step by step slowly, and agreeably too, till we got to the old, old days, where we called up all those scenes,—with you, Dora, the military balls, the pleasant nights, and pleasant days; what seemed like pictures or scenes out of a beautiful play seen in childhood — misty, indistinct, but delightful to think over. He spoke charmingly, regretfully, and even tenderly.

"Those were happy and innocent times," he said. "Scarcely happy after all for me, though there is a sort of happiness in such suffering. Yet compared with all I have gone through since——! Still in this life," he added, nodding at the cave behind us, "there is an excitement, too—it helps one to forget."

"But think, how will it end?" I said, with some excitement. "It cannot have the slow progress of what you call a life. It must hurry on suddenly to destruction. Oh, Grainger, stop, I implore of you, before it be too late! You have a dear immortal soul to save."

"But if it *be* too late," he said, "and was too late years ago? I don't know but if I saw any road—it all seems a jungle, or my eyes have got dim. Still, since you have talked to me, and brought before me those days, I don't feel quite so bad. We will speak of those things again—her name to me may have some power, at least, and if you will not think it a trouble or a bore while you *are* here——"

I wrung his hand warmly. "I would take it as a favour," I said; "oh, let me help you in some way, and if I *have* injured you, let me at least try and keep you

from this life, which must end in misery
and ruin."

" Well, we shall see," he said.

Two people came out of the cave a little
hurriedly. It was the youthful husband
walking first, by himself, his hands in his
pockets, his face flushed. She was tripping
behind him, with the most dismal, dejected
expression on her face. In a moment that
small hand, it had a tiny black mitten on,
was on his arm. It seemed to receive an
impatient welcome there, and dropped
again.

Grainger followed my eyes, " You see !"
he said, " the old story !"

Hers met mine, and they seemed to say,
" Oh, how right you were."

I knew I was—an instinct told me I
should be so. After all, bred in a country
town as I was, my dear Dora, I have
learnt to judge a little of human nature.

It comes by a sort of instinct. I wish I had been wrong in this view; but the same instinct whispers to me that this is but the end of the first act. Poor—poor little pair!

"That was the way it was with me at first," said Grainger; "I know that story pretty well. I have seen it here over and over again. Will you come in with me and see me try my hand—a new face, they say, brings new luck. And yet to-night it seems to jar upon me—you have brought me back into the old days. But still what can I do? As well tell a man who has sold himself to brandy, not to drink. Besides, what would be the use? I may as well finish, as I have begun. I have nothing to look to now."

"I cannot tell you how all this pains me, Grainger," I said, really distressed. "O, if my words could but have some little effect! Do—as you say the holy influence of the past is upon you—just for *this* night abstain. Even for Dora's sake, whom you once so loved, and who would rejoice to know that her name even had that little power left. If you knew its effect on *me!*"

A very curious look came into his face. He turned it off with a laugh. " Well, a night doesn't make much difference. I am a fool, I know. There, we'll walk about instead."

I felt almost a thrill of pleasure at this unexpected success. My pet's name is, indeed, an amulet to conjure with. After so many years, and at so many hundred miles' distance, to have such a power! And I think *I* may fairly claim a small share of the credit. Earnestness and sincerity go some way: perhaps, too, that little magnanimity. There was some little tact in my reception of him; others might have grown confused and angry. Here am I praising myself; but I am in such good spirits. But you must put up your gentle prayer for him, Dora.

CHAPTER XII.

I FOUND Grainger last night really entertaining and amusing. Hitherto a good
many of the people here have been like the
figures in front of the old grinding organs,
revolving, and glittering, and eccentric to
look at, but still without names or characters. Grainger knows them all, names,
dates, and addresses. *There* was the great
banker, there was the great speculator, the
man who could change paper into gold by
a touch, by a word even, and who was now
wandering about here, as poor as I or my
companion. Did I see that ascetical-look-
ing man? that was the Bishop of Graves-

end; or that woman in orange and black,
the famous Phryne Coralie,—English by
birth, but who had risen to the highest
rank in whatever "carrière" she followed.
There, too, was the great singer, who had
shrieked and declaimed — the tragedy
queens of opera, who had denounced the
craven Pollio many thousand nights in her
life, who had bearded wicked Counts de
Luna as many times more, who had sung
in the garden turning over the stage jewels
with grinning Mephistopheles and enraptured Faust; and here she was taking an
ice. Here on the terrace is the smaller
lady, who sits on a lower throne, but has
far more subjects and adorers. Here is
that little sycophant, known to every one
who comes to these places, who dogs lords
and ladies, and makes them stand while he
pours in his little adulatory small shot;
and here is quite a happy hunting ground

for those ladies of good connexion and title even, whose wings have been a little burnt as they fluttered through town drawing-rooms, but who find them quite sufficient to support them here, the atmosphere is so dense.

He is infinitely amusing is Grainger, his stories and his scandal, which I can quite conceive to be perfectly true. I can see he has got into spirits as he tells these things; and though it is rather light and unprofitable food, it takes off his mind from things more dangerous. What we said last night has left a deep impression: and to think of one so clever, so observant, so brilliant even, to have been shipwrecked in this way, indirectly through our doing! I must ask my dear pet to write me out something kind and sympathetic, which I can show to this poor waif and stray, and comfort him. That little heart has done the mischief, and she must make up a little, and I lay a husband's despotic commands on her. For I have set my heart on bringing this man back into the path of decency and order, and feel a conviction I *shall succeed*, if I could get but some power and influence over him. I say again, my pet must pray.

To-day is Sunday. How strange is a Sunday in this place! There is an English church, a chaplain, and a regular round of duty; but I think there would be less affectation in ignoring altogether such religious machinery. It is at variance with the place, quite an anachronism. For even in the relations of religion to the state—I mean to the "administration," they tell me there used to enter something grotesque the curious. When the use of the Lutheran church was graciously conceded to English worshippers it was an article

strictly insisted on, "that there should be
no preaching against going to the Bank"—
a pleasant euphuism for gambling. This
was a serious warning. Later on, as the
church and chaplain had to be kept up by
voluntary contributions and "a book,"
which was sent round to the visitors, the
company found that this was telling a little
indirectly on their interests. Testy fathers
grew impatient at these applications: "infernal begging place," "have to pay my
own man at home" — complaints which
were, of course, nothing to the Bank. But
when it was added, "I shall take care *not
to come back here again*," it took quite
another shape. Like the "refait" at their
own game, it told, on the whole, against
the player. So it was conveyed to the
chaplain that in their zeal for the advance-
ment of religion the administration would
be happy to pay him his salary, and a

handsome one too; that the collecting by a
book was scarcely dignified, gave him too
much trouble, &c. This tempting offer
was at once declined, and without reluc-
tance; but it was a *little too* strong. The
wages of preaching to be furnished by the
wages of sin! By-and-by, too, it might
have been required that a word or two
should be delicately insinuated in favour of
the harmlessness of the game. What a
place! If it should be my destiny to in-
sert the small end of the wedge, that is to
split—crack the whole institution asunder!
Already I see their servants — the hired
bullies of the place—looking at me with
distrust.

CHAPTER XIII.

Thursday.—I have not yet heard from Frankfort, but they tell me here that the merchant is away at his estates. There is no hurry, however—nay, I should wish for a little time to devote myself to my mission, as I may call it. I really feel a sort of "call" to do good here. I have watched Grainger all this day, and he has not gone in—at least I have not seen him myself; for I must keep to my fixed rule of not entering that cruel spiders' net, that tigers' den. I asked him this evening, had he kept his promise. He laughed, and would give me no answer. "Don't expect miracles," he said; "you can't expect a man to reform all at once. That little picture we made out together last night is still going about with me, dancing before my eyes. I wish I could shut it out; I did so for some years. Come in," he added, " and let us at least look at them, as the hungry beggars find some relief in looking into a cook-shop window."

I shook my head. " I have made a sort of resolution," I said, " and must keep to it. It would be sanctioning, in some sort, what I cannot approve."

" What rubbish!" he said, suddenly turning on me, then checked himself. " I beg your pardon; I have not got rid of my old ways as yet. I wish I had had those scruples. Talk to me now about her—about Dora—Mrs. Austen, I mean. It is like Annot Lyle and her harp."

These little allusions and turns of expres-

sions which dotted over all Grainger's conversation, with many others that I cannot
recal, show what a cultivated taste he had.
I did not give him credit for being so entertaining and amusing. We dined together
that day, and again we strayed back to the
old subject.

"The night," he said, "when I got that
news, is one I cannot dare to look back to.
It makes my head unsteady; you know the
feeling. Here, kellner, cognac! That's the
only thing."

"No," I said, "it is *not* the only thing;
it is as dangerous as the other. Forgive me
if I advise you again. I am going to have
some sherry, and oblige me by taking some
of it instead."

He groaned, laughed a little roughly, as
his habit was, and said:

"Well, I suppose so. No cognac, then.
What on earth is all this? You are making

me do things that no other man could at-
tempt."

" I have no power," I said, looking down.
" I am working with another charm."

He paused. " Ah, yes; I suppose that
is so."

I had already come to know the clergyman of the place. He had sent me his book,
and I suspect some of the gamblers' money
figured there to a good amount. I met this
gentleman in the evening, and he came up
to speak to me. There was something about
him I did not like, and he had an authori-
tative air which I was inclined to resent.
(I hear my Dora protest, who believes in
clergymen to the very bottom of her gentle
heart, and, I suspect, imagines that, with
their coats, shovel hats, white ties, &c., they
have come down ready dressed straight
from heaven; have a sort of angelic con-
formation underneath, wings folded up, &c.)

"I see," he said, sitting down next me on one of the green garden chairs—"I see you are intimate with that man here, Mr. Grainger, or Captain Grainger, as he calls himself. May I ask, do you know what his character is?"

I was happy to answer him with both facts and logic.

"The War Office also calls him captain," I said; "and I *do* know a good deal about him."

"I am afraid nothing good, then; for it is my duty to warn you, as a sort of temporary parishioner, the care of whose soul I have, that his character is very bad indeed, and that he is not a person any one of reputation should be seen with. He is a most dangerous man. You are young and inexperienced, Mr. Austen, and he has led several, as young and experienced, into mischief already. That is the reason I speak to you."

I could not help smiling.   This rustic clergyman, fetched out of some outlying district to this doubtful duty, lecturing *me* and others!   It was, of course, *in* his duty, and he meant well; but I think it was *rather* free and easy to a mere stranger.

"I am quite capable of taking care of myself, Mr. Lewis," I said.   "I have my own reasons for associating with that gen- tleman.   What if I succeeded in influencing *him* in changing his life and heart; does *that* at all enter into your philosophy?"

"Oh, well and good.   If you think you can do it," he said, smiling.   "God forbid I should interfere.   But we must judge these things by the ordinary rule of the world.   Have you any reason to lead you to hope?"

"Yes," I said, "I think I can do it." See his implied sensitiveness here—jealousy almost.

" Well, then, you ought to go and look after him now; for I was passing from the news-room just now, and saw him playing frantically. Come with me, and I will show him to you."

" I never go into that place," I said, coldly, and meaning a rebuke, "on *any* pretext."

" Into the news-room?" he said. "Why not? Ah, you have not patience to wait for the papers. It's a very good school for patience."

" As you ask me the reason, I do not wish to be indebted to men who fatten on human misery. They serve us their papers out of the monies they rob. I make no merit of it, but I think it better not."

" This sounds very strange," he said. " Let me ask, do you know the Bishop of Gravesend? He goes there every day. Do you know the good Lord Calborough, who

takes the chair at Meetings. I have seen
him looking over shoulders at the roulette.
Ah, I see you distrust yourself. Well, if
you are weak, there is no disgrace in flying
from the danger."

I have always resented this sort of superior knowledge of us which some clergymen affect, much as a doctor says, " Ah,
I know—feel a pain *here*—exactly—a sense
of fluttering after meals—exactly so." It
rather nettled me. I had heard, too, he was
rather sarcastic, and was said to know the
world. Then, I can tell him, he didn't
know *me*. Afraid to trust myself! I might
have been afraid to trust *him*, but not myself.

He went away. I was hardly inclined to
accept what he said about the Bishop of
Gravesend or the apostolic Lord Calborough.
Still he spoke with authority and with an
air of circumstance.

What was that pattering on the glass overhead? Rain, rain, coming down in pailfuls. There was a general *sauve qui peut* from the gardens. There they come rushing up the steps, eager, laughing, chattering like monkeys—creatures which, in other respects, some of the men resemble. All, of course, ascend, and go pouring into the cave. The bountiful rain, here, is unconsciously one of the faithful friends and servants of the administration. They should put him in their gew-gaw livery—green, gold, and scarlet, in which they dress up their disguised " bullies," who prowl about the room, ready to rush up on the slightest signal of a disturbance. I am almost alone on the terrace—a place of which I am getting tired. " Afraid to trust myself." I can't put that self-sufficient clergyman's speech out of my head. Thus it is with some natures: when they leap to a conclusion, it is always sure to be the meanest one that can present itself.

After all, I have made no *vow*, and am bound by no promise; nor do I, *more than the Bishop of Gravesend or my Lord Calborough*, think it any harm to go through those rooms, or even to linger there for some good object, provided your behaviour is not to be construed into an *endorsement* or approbation of the proceedings. I am no casuist, and there is a good broad band of common sense, I flatter myself, running through my composition. I would not be tied down as a weaker mind, by an abstract adherence to the mere *letter* of a resolution; I would look entirely to the spirit; and therefore, to assert this principle, I rise from my solitude on the terrace and walk into the cave. I wish to find Grainger.

CHAPTER XIV.

IT is a busy time indeed. There is clatter, rattle, click-click, sudden pause, almost awful, a low proclamation, added to the setting in of chink and jingle. Such crowds—half a dozen deep about the table; while outside promenade as thickly, the well-dressed girls and ladies; the stupid men who are pouring into pretty ears their insipid jests, but which they are not to be blamed for thinking racy from the hearty reception they meet; the eager and amused first visitors, delighted and confounded with everything, and chuckling with a stupid complacency over the privilege of being allowed to enjoy those lights and gorgeous chambers, soft sofas, and amusement, all *for nothing!* There are mean minds to whom this element is a sort of whet. (I hear my dear pet at home say, as she reads, that I am getting a little bitter; but this place *does* help to give one a mean estimate of human nature.)

I look round and try to make out Grainger. I wander from one table to the other. Certainly on this night of excitement there can be no such study as these human faces and expressions, especially at the moment *the cards are being dealt.* Not at chapel or church, if the *Doctor Seraphicus* himself were preaching, could we find five seconds of such absorbed expectancy and attention. The heart, soul, all, are in the faces. Suddenly, as the verdict sounds— light, positive light, drifts over some, and a positive shadow over others. Shocking,

shocking, yet so interesting! Talk of a play! I could look on here from morning to night. It has endless variety, and I must be very strait-laced if I could not do so with that object, the study of human character merely, in view. By the way, the doctor said I was to relax, and amuse myself in every way. I suppose *he* meant to gamble, but that prescription, my good quack, won't do for me. I have certainly been moping a little.

There I see a greater crowd—faces all looking at one face, gutteral whispers— "way"—so the Germans call "oui"—"Zay luay!" I can understand—a hero of the night: a worn, lorn creature, a sad, high-browed, bald, gentlemanly man, fighting the desperate fight, standing up to the very teeth of the bank. He was playing what seems the forlorn hope—"*le maximoom*," twelve thousand francs every time; and a

fat, clean, snowy cushion of notes was before him, delicately marked in faint blue,
and as thick as the leaves of a book.   On
this night, Mephistopheles is playing one
of his most cruel freaks, and one which he
is very fond of.   This votary has been
winning during the previous few days, and,
it is said, has carried off some six or eight
thousand pounds.   The pinch-faced eccle-
siastical-looking overseer walks about uneasily, and has regarded him with dislike
all but openly expressed.   But to-night I
can see the bale of notes shifting across
from one colour to the other, ruthlessly
seized on, counted over with an ostenta-
tious particularity, note after note laid out
in splendid piles, and the trifling balance
tossed back contemptuously.   Then I see
him gathering up his dwindling notes, turn
them over with a pitiable irresolution,
and again lay them down on another

colour. Again is proclamation made; away
they flutter, drawn in by the merciless far-
stretching croupier's claw; and I see the
yellow fingers working nervously at his
forehead, which is as yellow. Then comes
the sudden scrape, as the chair is pushed
back, and he is gone. No one cares for the
unsuccessful, and no eye of sympathy, rather
a look of impatient contempt, follows him.

But Grainger. Then it was my eye fell
upon him, seated close by, a few gold
pieces before him, his face distorted with
impatience, fury, and hate. Indeed, it
seemed another Grainger, or that a new
soul had entered into him. It almost
startled me; but still I recollected what I
had laid out for myself. I went round
softly and touched him: he looked back
savagely.

"Well?" he said; "what the devil is
it now?"

"Come away, do; I want to speak to you."

"Is that all? Well, I don't want to be worried now."

" Do listen to me, Grainger. Come away, do."

"Con*found* it, leave me alone, will you? What the devil do you mean?"

Such demoniac fury! The clergyman was right after all. I had been only deceiving myself, and with a bitter disappointment I turned away. In an instant I was attracted by a sudden confusion and din of voices, all speaking together.

I looked back. There was Grainger standing up, his arms swinging, and gesticulating; his mouth pouring out angry French. Three croupiers were as vehemently expostulating, and pointing, and emphasising with their rakes. They have not paid him, he says. They have cheated—swindled him! The "gallery," as they call the people standing round, take different sides; and now steals up, as if from behind a tree, that methodist-looking inspector, whose skin is drawn so tight, and whose clothes are so brushed—by machinery I think. He quietly whispers Grainger, no one can learn what he says; but I see his head nodding like the bill of a sparrow. That man's soul, I suspect, is as tight as his skin and clothes. I suppose he is worth his six or seven hundred a year to the administration. What he says seems to awe Grainger—already the gamblers are impatient at all this *tapage* about a few wretched Louis, when there are hillocks of gold, metallic ant-hills, rising all over the table.

The croupier seizes the moment. The cards are being dealt, and after *that* there can be no more "row." Here again Mephistopheles and his crew have such an advantage. For in analogous relations, a crowd is sure to take part with one of themselves; but no one here knows what the next coup may bring, and in that expectancy, selfishness grows impatient and sides with the bank. I admire the dexterity with which the meaner human passions are thus turned to profit, and every little broil composed.

I turn away not a little disgusted. Certainly the strangest and most dramatic of scenes, and not unprofitable to study. See here, for instance, a little dingy shopwoman, with her two children over yonder on the sofa—perhaps sells candles and tobacco; in her brown thread gloves she has her " little florin." The dull anxiety in her German face is surprising. Down goes the piece on " manque," and I see her look away as the ball spins round. Her heart, I am sure, almost stops. She hears, but does not see, the result. The smile of delight is exquisite—she tries again—again succeeds—and again succeeds. Now she is over at the sofa showing her three prizes lying in the brown thread gloves. How she has clutched at them over the shoulder of the genteel sitting player, and who shakes her off impatiently, and half gives an execration. *He* has forty Louis before him; but she was afraid that if she was not prompt, he or some other greedy player would seize on her little treasure. Then she returns to the table full of triumph, flushed with victory. She watches and waits a favourable opportunity; but Mephistopheles has seen her with one of his grins. She loses her first piece; a palpable agony flits across her face. She tries again. Zero! Her little piece is in prison; something like agony is in that dull face. The next turn, it is gone. She is trying again, but will lose. Oh, if she had been only *content to remain as she was!* The very air must be dense with ejaculations of this sort, wrung from a thousand disappointed hearts.

Over yonder I see the young wife sitting disconsolate, and with such a wistful look towards the table. She is waiting for *him.* He is playing — Mephistopheles needn't trouble himself about *that* business. It is in fair train of itself, and will move on to his wishes, of its own motion.

As I go out on the cool terrace some one touches my arm.

"I owe you a hearty apology," Grainger said, "for my roughness. Once we begin there, we lose all restraint."

I answered coldly, "that it was no matter."

"But it *is* matter," he said, angrily; "I gave you a right to speak to me, and I met you most unworthily. I had some excuse, for the interruption brought about the row that you saw. I suppose your well-meant caution cost me only ten louis; but say you are not angry."

There was something very winning in his manner, and I could not resist him.

"But I thought you were going to give all this up?" I said. "You led me to hope I had some influence."

"Ah! my dear fellow, that is very well for you, but not for me. I declare I wonder at you, at times, to see you so steady in the midst of all this temptation."

"My dear Grainger," I answered, "I am as weak as you, I dare say; but I *have* a little secret—a prescription."

"What do you mean?"

"Well, habitual self-restraint: a sort of indifference also (for I don't want to take any undue credit): and the greatest of all—*Prayer.* Oh, Grainger, say that I can't, if you will, but aid from above——"

"Oh yes, of course. We know that," he said, brusquely. Still I saw he was impressed. The seed *might* be in the ground.

CHAPTER XV.

DURING our absence a strange metamorphosis had taken place in the gardens. They had become perfectly crammed, and below us was a dense mass of moving figures, but now all lit up. In the daytime I had noted trees dotted about, that seemed like palm-trees with drooping branches. It was a rare "administration" device to line these with gas-pipes, and hang white globes over them, up and down. When they treat our poor human nature as they do, it is only all of course that they should deal with the glorious fruits of the earth in the same fashion. Gas and paint, and gilding and gewgaws, these make up *their* sunlight, and grass greens, and variegated colours of nature. To the fresh breath of heaven, they prefer the miasma of their crowded gaming-room. I dare say M. D——, the superintendent, finds it suits his lungs better than the most bracing mountain atmosphere, and I suppose goes to Baden or Spa for his holiday. However, here I see the whole garden lit up with these trumpery illuminated gas arches and stars, and meagre hearts, and such things, and the crowd amused and delighted like children as they are. *Qu'il est beau! Vraiment c'est magnifique!* And how generous and liberal this administration! "*And all for nothing,*" says old paterfamilias — the same who sits on the *Times* while he reads the *Daily News,* and little dreams that his eldest, Charles, has already paid to this generous board some five-and-twenty napoleons "on the red," which alone would defray the cost of several of these festivities. But when the band begins the last galop with *éclat* and animation, and some half a dozen cheap Bengal lights are stuck in the trees, poor innocent trees! and made to fizz and blaze, then the enthusiasm bursts out; a perfect roar of childish delight rises, and we hear again how "*beau*," how "*magnifique*" this conduct is on the part of the administration. I am far from joining in these praises; I think the whole shabby and contemptible to a degree—with their few jets of gas, and their newspapers, and their chairs, for which nearly every one has to pay more or less handsomely. Nay, I have discovered that there is not a young girl, the most blushing, blooming, and innocent, who comes here, that does not coax papa for three florins or so, "just to try my luck, my dear," and which is swept into the hands of these monsters. Even Thomas, the valet, and poor Cox, the ladies' maid, they have stolen up and contributed their two hard-earned gulden. Ah, M. D——, with the pinched nose and the drum-tight skin, decent and respectable as you are, *gérant en chef* of the company, or whatever you call yourself, do you think that if we had you in England, you would not be committed for trial summarily, or that your correct demeanour would go to influence the verdict of the jury? This fellow, I can see, observes the look of dislike with which I measure him—there is a *rapport* in these things as well as in likings —and I can see he is thinking, " You are coming into our net, my boy; we shall strip you, and that will teach you not to be offensive to the administration. You want a lesson !"

When I was talking to Grainger last night

on the only subject on which he can talk fluently, a short stumpy man with a jet, glossy, hairdresser beard and moustache, a little hat, and coat very short, came up and said languidly, "How do, Grainger?" He sat down in front of us, leant back, drawing at his cigar with half-closed eyes, and moving his cane up and down between his knees, in a sort of slow dance.

"Uncommon bad, D'Eyncourt," said Grainger; "I went back to those infernal tables, in spite of the advice of my good friend here, which I had determined to follow——"

"Pretended to determine to follow," he answered with a slow drawl. "Tell the truth always, and shame—your friend in- side."

I never saw a face I disliked more; it was so tallowy, and then the little eyes were quite flat and oval, and exactly of the pattern we see in a pig. I was going to say "cat," but the head had not the character which a cat has. He had a sort of Turkish air, and I had often remarked him as he looked at ladies passing by, with an inert blinking, as though he were saying, "I could bring *you* to me, if I chose to exert myself; you could not resist, but you are not worth it." He was a solitary man, though sometimes I saw him seated with a family of girls about him, his head back, his pig's eyes blinking at them, the words dropping languidly from his mouth, as who should say, "I just serve you out a few marbles, you are not worth more, and mind—I am doing this to amuse myself."

He had been a traveller, and the glossy locks were said to take a good deal of time to keep in that rich and glossy state.

"You say very queer things," said Grainger. "Only that we know you——"

" No, you don't; I want no excuse of that sort. I say whatever I like. And as for people knowing me, it makes no difference."

" Then some one will be thrashing you one of these days."

The only answer was a sleepy look of contempt, which seemed to make Grainger uneasy.

" My friend here," he said, " believes in systems ; my friend Austen—who has come here for his health."

The other never looked at me a second, or seemed to acknowledge this ambiguous introduction.

" Well, *you* have always played on a system," he drawled out, " and with such success !"

" I never lost, but when I did. Curse them all! They are the devil's own mouse-traps and spring-guns."

" You know best about *him*," said the

other. "But you have stumbled on a truth for once—and of course too late. You point a moral *here;* the good show you to their sons as a warning. If I was the administration, I'd pay you to go away, or to keep out of sight."

"You speak to me in a very strange way. If I didn't owe you a trifle of money——"

"Then say nothing about it, as the situation must continue."

I felt, indeed, for Grainger; there was something so studied in this insolence; and I could not resist whispering a question, "Is it a large sum?"

A rueful nod was the reply, and a smile, a dull smile, melted over the tallow face.

"And so you have taken up a system— the last resource? Well, well."

"I did not say *I* had," replied Grainger. "My friend here, Mr. Austen, believes in it. Let me introduce him, Mr. D'Eyncourt."

Grainger seemed to find some revenge in this little stroke. I was provoked, for I did not wish to know this man.

"Pray what is your system?" he said, without looking at me.

"I have nothing of the kind; only I noticed that everybody who lost to-night seemed to play very wildly, now on this, now on that, without any guide."

"And pray what is the guide *you* have found out?"

"There can be nothing that you can call a *guide*; but it seems to me common sense that if one colour has been coming up a great many times, we may naturally begin to look out for the other."

"Oh, *that* is common sense is it?" he said, taking his cigar out of his mouth. "It may be so; I never pretend to say what is common sense or not. Still there are thousands who have thought of what you have said, absolutely thousands; in fact, every beginner *invariably* makes that discovery, after he has won three or four florins."

"You quite mistake. I am no beginner, and have won no florins."

"Well, say a napoleon. It is the regular speech—the regulation discovery. Take my advice, keep your napoleon, and let your system go."

"I really do not understand," I said coldly. "I have never played, and with the grace of Heaven never *shall* indulge in what I think utterly wrong and sinful, and the most demoralizing pastime ever introduced upon this earth!"

That was plain speaking, Dora. He looked at me curiously. "I have nothing of course to do with that. You are in the church, I see."

"But taking the mere theory," I went on, "I am right. I know something of mathematics—of the common chances of everyday life, and every man of science will tell you that a rule is better than no rule."

"Oh, you are wrong, my dear Austen," said Grainger; "utterly. Your man of science is quite a donkey in these matters. It is one of the invariable delusions of this place. You will find out in time."

"Well, look at this card," I said, warmly, "which I marked as the game went on— from curiosity, just to test the thing."

"From curiosity, just to test the thing," said D'Eyncourt. "Yes."

"Well, see, it falls into the shape—exactly as I said. There is a proof."

"Oh! the card and pin," said he, with an air of superiority I could have struck him for. "Everybody appeals to *that*. Really this uniformity is delicious."

"Come away, Grainger," I said, feeling I

could hardly control myself.   "I am tired, let us have some supper."

As we walked away, Grainger said, "My dear friend, he's right.   You can't understand these things so well.   Your experience don't go beyond a sixpenny roulette table on a race-course.   But here we do things *en grand*, you see."

"I am right," I said coldly, "though I do know nothing about even a sixpenny roulette."

"I *wish* you were.   Well, when do you go over to Frankfort?"

When we got home I found a letter on the table from the German gentleman.   He has at last returned, and will see me to-morrow morning.   This looks like business. No letter for some days from my pet, which makes me a little uneasy.   Not that I shall be troubled.   For I use these little "trials of the third class," as I call them, as so many opportunities for wholesome discipline, for keeping the mind straight and steady, hardening it to imaginary woes, strengthening and giving a tone to the judgment. I am right also, in my judgment, whatever that languid upstart may think.

CHAPTER XVI.

Wednesday.—I almost think we strangers are a little careless in the way we talk about what is the chief feature of this curious place. If I was one of the truly scrupulous, which I *would* be, only that I am so afraid of lapsing into cant and censoriousness—I should watch every single word. There are so many who from not thinking over the danger, as I do, are surprised into mischief. Hunting men tell me they have seen mere boys "go at" desperate jumps, which they, with better horses and better experience, would shrink from. I do not boast, nor am I full of self-confidence — Heaven knows! But I keep my eyes open, and scan the country. Thus at dinner, when I hear the light talk (and how it *does* recur to that one subject!) there is the usual "Were you at the rooms?" "Yes, just dropped in before dinner, and had a shy at the red. Knocked my half-dozen Friedrichs out of 'em." And then the hand rattles money in the pocket, which so unaccountably seems to me to be always accepted as a convincing *proof* of having won. But observe this touch of nature. Every one knows there is so much falsehood about these boasts, that he knows he is suspected for being in the atmosphere of the place; and he knows besides that he is telling what is not true. I could swear that the "half-dozen Friedrichs" were two: but in our vulgar elation here, we must exaggerate. Thus I trace indirectly to the infernal system, lying and

swaggering—germs of worse vices.   When
the careless boast is made, I look round
the table to the faces near me, who are all
turned, listening and admiring, their fork
half lifted, descending again, to two very
pretty and interesting girls' faces, over which
steals that wistful, semi-greedy look, which
I note in this place floats about like an evil
angel.   I look to the right, and see the
face of an honest Eton boy, browned with
exercise, and *he* is listening.   His expression is one of *knowing* resolve; *i.e.*, " When
the governor is hard and fast with his
Times, I'll drop in.   I don't see why I
can't do as well as that man !"   Governor
himself, hale and rubicund, who six weeks
before has looked sternly through his
glasses (sitting in his parlour) at an itine-
rant roulette-player, and given him " six
weeks," is smiling indulgently.   " You
have made a good thing of it, sir.   Take

care you don't burn your fingers." This about the " six weeks," is a fact, I believe, and occurred. But see how the thing works. That careless speech, untrue and boastful, sows seed abroad: in a day or two the vile tares will be coming up in those innocent flower beds.

On such an occasion I try and do what I can to stop the mischief—generally with a poor result, I am not ashamed to confess. Still there is the good intention. Some of our missionary friends would say, " Of course you reproved them, and quoted the sacred text." Nothing of the kind—nothing so injudicious, though I dare say I could have improved the occasion quite as well. I think I know human nature something better than those gentry, who seem to me always to blunder as to fitting times and seasons. Now, how do I act? I say in a cheerful way, that it is notorious that it is

11—2

quite hopeless fighting against the Bank.
No one ever wins but two classes—the
great and desperate players, or the players
who don't care to lose. Some one says
scornfully, "Why, there was Macgregor
here last year paid all his expenses
and bagged eighty Friedrichs." Paid all
his expenses!—the invariable phrase. See
the meanness, the shabbiness of what is
underneath that speech. Fancy an English gentleman at home, boasting after a
night's whist, that he had paid for his
train and his hotel bill and cab hire! I en-
trap Mr. Macgregor's friend at once. "Ah,
but he was a cautious player—watched
the turns." "Nothing of the kind; flung
down when and where he liked!—money's
no object to him." "Precisely," I said,
smiling, "then he falls within one of my
classes. Is he coming this year, again?"
"I believe so." "Well then, if I betted, I

would wager that he will lose not only all that he won last year, but more than a similar amount of his own.

This conversation was at one of the table d'hôtes at the hotel of the Beautiful View, where the dining life becomes so pleasant, and where every one comes in in good humour and hungry, save only some of the poor foolish moths who have burnt a hole in the edge of their wings just before dinner. How bright the faces!—what spirits among the young girls!—what anticipation! —what gaiety!—what chatter! Cares, troubles, business even, is all lying away at home, locked-up with the dockets in the safes and cupboards. I like to see the florid, stout, grey-whiskered, double eye-glassed father who pays so gallantly for all, even for the vast load of chests and boxes which must go always on a cart. I like the way he enjoys the meal, and good-

naturedly allows that this "Assmanshausen" or "Förster Cabinet" is "really a
capital good wine." The waters are doing
him good too, and he is disposed to allow
that, for a place *not* English, a very fair at-
tempt indeed has been made to smooth over
the foreign absurdities.

I fancy they like talking with me—young
men and young girls—I suspect because
they fancy I am an expert as to the great
excitement of the place; know all its secrets
from having lost a whole fortune in the
service.

Is not this amusing, and not unnatural
also, for I am always adroitly insinuating
something the company of speculators would
not thank me for? If they knew the mischief my little mission work, as I may call
it, is doing their nefarious trade! I often
think if M. D——, the cat-like, knew what I
was about, he would ask me to dine at his

charming villa in the most friendly way, and when we were alone, after a choice bottle had been set on, would lay his hand on my arm, and say, " My dear friend, we are both men of the world, you perhaps more so than I am, for in this bank of ours I really live as if shut up in a monastery. Now let us understand each other. You are costing us so much—come, don't tell me: we hear everything; for how much *shall I fill up this?* With an enemy of *esprit* and such *finesse* we must deal generously. Would two hundred pounds pay your expenses home?" I smile at this picture; and yet if I were to calculate all the people I have talked with, and "tot up" the value of such little impressions as I have made, I think the loss to the bank, thus represented, would not be far short of what I have said. I know the answer, however, which M. D——should receive from me, in spite of his good wine and his domestic wife and family.

As I say, they all listen to me at dinner as to an expert. "How *do* you find these things out?" says a very child-faced girl to me, with a pleasant wonder. "I am no mystery man," I answer; "a little thought, a little watching, reveals everything. I have reason to know that the bank obtains seventy-five per cent. of its winnings from the stray gentlemen of the time; ten pounds from this, twenty from that, fifty from a third, a hundred from a fourth. The professed gambler gives them back their own money: he only takes up time and room. But it is not, after all, with you and me they are playing, but with human nature, and with poor *weak* human nature. We cannot even conceive the familiars, those croupiers let loose the moment the innocent put down their money for the first time. They come rushing up like touts at a railway station."

I saw a smile on some of the youths' faces, but the child-like girl was listening with a devotional expression. "Well, sir?" says Paterfamilias, who, I believe, secretly wishes to pick up a hint about winning from what I was talking about. "Bear with me a moment," I said; "you will know their presence by one simple test. You," I said, turning to the young girl, "may have won your one florin the other day, and you were delighted—thought it a fortune." "Exactly," she said, eagerly; "papa put down for me."

"Suppose you go on next day and win three more. Then luck turns; they slip away one by one, and you come to dinner here with only one florin left. Now compare that stage with your first. You were excited, enraptured then; now you are dispirited and dejected and *uneasy*. Mark the word. Yet you had a florin then, and you have a florin now."

"Ah!" the young girl says, "if I had but followed papa's advice, and gone away with my four florins!"

I could not help smiling.

"You see," I said, "I can guess pretty well in these things. Well, here is the secret of this difference of humour. You are thinking of *what you have lost*, though you have literally lost nothing. Multiply that by Friedrichs, and we have the feeling of the greater gamester. He looks on every loss of what he has won as a loss from his capital, though properly it belongs to another, and has been only lent to him. Believe me, this restless dissatisfaction is the grand paid familiar of these speculators, and does all their work for them."

Paterfamilias, I see, is interested.

" 'Pon my word, sir, there is a great deal of truth in what you say. But how on earth did he find out about you, Polly?— And see here, William, my boy, I forbid you to put down another kreutzer."

" They wont let him do that, papa," says the young girl, eagerly.

" Well, I know nothing about their rules, and don't want to. But mind, William, don't let me see you in those blackguard rooms again. It's ungentlemanly, so it is— a set of sharpers."

I can see that the young fellow's heart is in the " blackguard" rooms already. But the father is a good-natured old fellow, and is loved by his children; so that in my little unpretending way I may have saved a good and domestic family from trouble, discord, disobedience, and demoralization. I could have given paterfamilias a little hint himself; for outsiders who saw a respectable English country gentleman putting down, even for his daughter, would be affected by the example.

CHAPTER XVII.

Friday. — I have just returned from Frankfort. Such a charming old town, refreshing to see in all its reverend innocence and hoariness, after the flaunting garishness of this new and wicked spot. I saw the merchant, who received me very graciously, and had lunch ready. After it was over, we talked of business, and he began by saying that he had determined to give the sum he had offered before, and no more. Something prompted me at that moment to try and do something for my friend, and *act* a little, though I now doubt if it was strictly conscientious. Still, making a bargain *is* making a bargain—does not our conventional morality hold it to be a mere trial of skill—and I boldly said that it was too little, quite out of the question, &c. He was a Jew, and I think not disappointed that there was to be some "haggling." On that we set to work; my pet should have seen the latent diplomatic powers I called into play. Will you believe me—if I *did* not actually triumph over the Jew in the end, and obtain a hundred pounds more for my friend! A memorandum was signed, and a day named for me to go before the consul, and finally conclude the matter. I am greatly elated at this little victory.

On coming home, I found Grainger waiting at the train. My first impulse was to tell him of what I had done; but a wiser discretion checked me. Here again is a little discipline; and it seems to me, on analysis, that this wish of communicating news, &c., is nothing more than a mere shape of vanity, and does not arise from any desire to gratify or amuse any one else. He told me he had not played the whole day, but that he had amused himself *watching* the game in *my* fashion, and trying whether there was anything in what I had said.

"Well, I spent two hours in that way," he said, "and, my dear friend, I must give it against you. Our friend the Pasha, as you called him, is right. You really don't know what that man knows."

"He is a shallow creature, I know," I said; "I wonder how he is even tolerated here."

"Well, he has a history, I can tell you. Harems and seraglios, and sacks and all that. Romantic to a degree."

"Romantic," I said, angrily; "that is

the genteel name for vice and villany and rascaldom."

"Hush! there he is. I mustn't abuse him, as he has me bound—1 mean I mustn't let him *hear* me abuse him."

D'Eyncourt came up, his head back, his round hat back also, and with a little pink on the centre of his "mutton-fat" cheeks.

"Well," he said, "going in to play—to step into the birdlime, and try a system?"

"I can't play," said Grainger. "I am going to give up for ever. It will be a struggle, but it's all for the best."

"What! going to reform? How many tricks have you tried in your life, my friend? Is this to be the last?"

"Tricks, Mr. D'Eyncourt?" said Grainger, colouring. "Tricks?"

The other put his head further back, as if to get a good look, and said, coldly, "I repeat, *tricks*, Mr. Grainger."

The other, muttering something to himself, looked down. I felt for him.

"Yes, I always speak plain. Will you come in, and let us look at the game. D'ye hear?"

"No use asking you, Austen," said Grainger, as it were obeying an order; "and I wont press you to come. I shall only be one moment."

He looked very helpless and appealingly at me.

"Oh, I forgot," said D'Eyncourt; "you mentioned something about scruples. Then stay with your friend. There's Colonel Manby yonder. He'll do."

I had already, my pet will remember, rather qualified the resolution I had taken about going into the rooms. Looking at it in *that* way, I believe, we are not responsible, in any sort, for the doings of the wicked—at least as regards mere indifferent actions. As well might we look into the lives of all friends jealously, and "cut" every one of them—fathers, brothers, who had done anything that was not quite correct. I said:

"I have no scruples of the kind. Merely walking through, or looking on, does not affect the question."

We entered. High play was going on; the Count with the worn face was in his place, his little bale of clean notes before him.

"Ah, there he is!" said D'Eyncourt. "They have got their pigeon. Let me see; how many feathers has he left? Just a few, but enough to play with. Yes, they are giving him two or three back, to stick into his wing if he can."

There was a crowd opposite, uttering the usual ejaculations—much as what the lower Irish do when a strange story is told to

them: " Il a gagné," " C'est le max-i-moom"
—so they pronounce it. " Fooah ?" the
breath being drawn in slowly between the
teeth.

"The old story," said D'Eyncourt, contemptuously.

> " Only begin,
> And then win ;
> *That's* their ruse
> To make you lose ;—

a little gambling proverb of my own. A
pity he should be told of the new system."

I had been watching the player, and an
idea occurred to me. I snatched a card and
a pin. I know all this will amuse my pet.
It is a duty, surely, to give a lesson, now
and again, to the foolish. It is serving the
world and society, and God knows, very
cheaply. Yon Missionary would keep outside, and gather up his gown.

" Now," I said, coolly, " what if I tell

you how he ought to play to win? What
will you say to my common sense then?"

"What will I say to *your* common sense?
I am sure I can't tell."

"You shall be told, then; and you be a
witness, Grainger."

Red had come up three times.

"Now," I said, "let him put on black."

"Oh no," said Grainger.   "Don't you
see—he is going for the run."

"Well, what does this gentleman say?"
I said to D'Eyncourt.

"Nothing," he answered; "why should
I say anything?"

The player *did* "go for the run," and
with his "maximum;" but away it fluttered
to the green leathern tomb of the Capulets,
the slab of which shut down on it with a
fatal click.   I said nothing.

The player then waited until two deals
had intervened.

"Now," I said, "let him put on red, and he will certainly win."

He almost seemed to have heard me. Down went his maximum, pushed across with trembling fingers; and in a few seconds was heard the chant, " Rouge gagne, et couleur!"

I will not dwell on this, for fear of tiring my pet; but I will tell the whole scene to her later. But "suffice it to say," as the novelists are fond of repeating, I *really foretold* nearly every successful colour, and, by some mysterious *rapport*, the Count seemed to follow or anticipate every prophecy of mine.

" By heaven," said Grainger, in a strange excitement, "it's devilry or magic! For heaven's sake lend me, do, some one, three, naps—only three—one, then—one! Well, then," he added, piteously, " a double florin; you wont refuse that?"

"Recollect your promise," I whispered to him—"your resolution, your *solemn* resolution——"

"Folly !" he said; "you are robbing me at this moment; it is cruel of you."

I was watching D'Eyncourt. He was biting his lips with vexation. I could not resist saying,

"You would not admit my common sense," I said; "it is not to be expected."

"It is easy to play a game with a pin and a card. Back your opinion with money, and I'll do the same."

"I never play," I said coldly, "and never shall, please God. There are some whom it is hopeless to convince of the difference between a mere mathematical study, and a pursuit so dangerous, and deadly both to soul and body."

"Caution, religion, and *all* the theological virtues. Good. Now—just to show you how they affect me—there go my five louis on red."

" If you wait about twice more," I said, calmly, "you would have a better chance. I hardly think red could come up now."

"Rouge *perd*, et couleur," came before he could actually answer me. I went on.

" *Now* I dare say there might be a chance for you, if you would risk it——"

" I shall go on black," he said, putting down ten louis.

" Rouge gagne, et couleur!" was the verdict.

So it went on, I with a most extraordinary success in my guesses, being astray not more than three or four times; and when I showed my card, the pin-holes all certainly fell into the shape I had predicted. Mr. D'Eyncourt, however, had lost over fifty louis. It was his own doing.

" This comes," he said, " of playing with

people talking about you, pestering you
with systems and cards and pins.   There,
Manby—there's a gentleman here turned
prophet.   Perhaps he'll tell you something
about the Derby."

Before I could reply he was gone, and I
turned to Grainger.

" Your friend is inclined to be insolent,"
I said, " and I am not inclined to put up
with it.   Like any one who cannot bear to
be told they are in the wrong, or to be in
presence even of common sense, he wishes
to give vent to his own spleen and malice."

Grainger was hardly attending.

" Why didn't you let me?   I might have
been rich at this moment; I'd have made
three hundred louis in the wake of that
fellow.   I might have been free from *him*,
and, but for my slavery, I might have paid
my bill at the lodgings."

" Is it so much ?" I asked.

"Two hundred florins—a wretched sum. But he is insolent enough for it to be *ten thousand*."

"Is that all?" I said. "We are very poor, as you know, Grainger; but if a hundred florins will help, I can let you have that much; but you must solemnly swear —not a florin goes down on that green cloth. An oath on your Bible, mind."

"I'll swear anything," he said. "You are noble, and have always treated me nobly, whatever I may have said. Still," he added, suddenly, "you know it is not so heavy an obligation. You admit that? Only a few pounds, you know."

There was something in his tone that rather jarred on me; but I recollected that he was always subject to these alternations, passing from a most cordial, genial, and even softened tone, into a cold, bitter, and hostile manner. It was his way. He was

a disappointed man, so we must have al-
lowance.

Thus that day terminated.   Somehow
the calm country-town monotony of mind
which I had brought with me seems to
have given way a little before the whirl, as
it were, of this place—the strange figures,
the dramatic incidents, the curious motives
of this place.   But I am learning precious
lessons—oh, most precious lessons!   It is
like tonics and cold baths for the mind.
After all, how many of us go through life
without having even the *faintest* conception
of what is going on, no conception of what
attitudes, and motions, and wonderful
freaks the human mind is capable of.
Novels and plays tell us a good deal, but
we do not believe in them.   One day lets
in a flood of light worth a thousand of
Mudie's "sets."   Shall I own that I dwell
with complacency on the fact that I, a mere

rustic, ungraduated in the world's devices, should have "held my own" in that little scene to-day, by the sheer force of good plain sense and reason? Thank Heaven, I am growing better every hour! Heaven is very good to us, certainly.

CHAPTER XVIII.

Tuesday.—An interval of some days has passed without my writing a line. The fact is, the hours are running by so fast, and so many little events crowd into the day, that I find hardly time to do anything. I have even got a little backward in my letters to my pet. I have been making a sort of study of this mysterious and dangerous science of chances, which is luring all these poor souls to destruction. It is one of the most curious subjects of inquiry, and there can be no doubt that there is more in it than the common vulgar affectation of superior knowledge will admit.

If I could but freshen up my old mathematics, I could work the thing out regu-
larly. The doctor tells me that having
something of interest thus to amuse and
occupy the mind is the real secret of my
improvement. I could have told *him* that.

Shall I own to another discovery I have
made, viz., that when Mephistopheles is
playing for souls, he does it with tolerable
fairness. I constantly hear men, Englishmen too, going out with flushed faces, and
muttering " Pack of d—d swindlers—set of
cheats!" Now, a very narrow scrutiny
compels me to own that their dealings are
fair, or seem fair. Shall I go further, and
say that they really *seem* to put themselves
at a disadvantage with those they encounter. That, of course, is their business, not
mine. I spent *four* hours the other morning watching the game, and I suppose
riddled some half a dozen cards with pin-

holes.　The result was the same in *the main*. I begin to see the whole system like a revelation, adding to it, from experience, this rider: the splendid gift of *self-restraint*. *There* they all break down; they cannot halt in time, even for five minutes.　One would be tempted to go and whisper this simple recipe to each one of the poor dupes who are rushing down this fatal hill; but it is not *my* business.　*Quem Deus vult perdere*. *I* could not save them.

I see at these little seats of extortion— the stalls where they sell photographs and ornaments at literally double the price they can be had anywhere else—I see absolute treatises on the game.　One a serious volume at twenty francs; the others little handbooks at a franc, giving " a sure and infallible method for winning."　These little impostures were diverting from the solemn tables set out and the grand terms.　" The

intermittance," " series," and the oracular
advice. The qualities requisite for the
gambler are to be " courage, vigour, *élan*,
coolness, and insensibility." " System,"
above all, must be pursued (and so far I go
with him); "otherwise," he adds, gravely,
"you will indeed remain a simple *player*
(joueur), but you will never become *spécu-*
lateur." He fills pages with his various re-
cipes, but at the end announces that without a capital of some *four thousand florins*
you will not have "a secure base of opera-
tion to work from." And yet I see this
rubbish in the hands of many a poor fool;
and, what is more, I see many a greater
fool sitting industriously with his book and
two pencils, one red and one black, marking
the colours. One dreadful old fellow, who
is nearly blind, has a complete apparatus—
a little dial, mounted on a pincushion, and
bristling all over with red and black headed

pins, which he shifts about, and not for half an hour, perhaps, will the safe combination he so desires, arise, and then he plays his miserable florin. Of course he loses, as indeed I could have told him. I was almost tempted to lay my hand upon his arm and check him; but, as I have said so often, that is not my business. Oh, ship of fools, indeed! One might almost be in doubt whether to laugh at or weep over the poor blind souls who are going through the miserable pantomime of their own destruction with such gravity.

Sometimes I see an incident all but comic. The table is laden with gold and covered with billets, and the croupier touching each with the magic rake, repeating aloud the sums staked. " L'or va au rouleau!" (This always in a growl, as who should say, " We have you.") " Vinsang louis au beelyet!" (This in a mournful manner of expostulation, as who should say, "Why not *all* the Beelyet?") And "Muttyez à la masse!" (This very sharp and short, like the click of a trigger before firing.) An humble fellow has laid down his double-Frederick, a good stake, but modest, seeming more than it is among the surrounding magnificence. The dealer is about to begin, when, in a fit of compunction, the man calls out, "Moitié à la masse!" and causes a perfect roar in the gallery. Yet these men had their hundred and two hundred louis, their "maximoom" even, depending on the deal. So they laughed and went to play, when the guillotine was at its hardest work.

The gardens are getting dull enough; I grow tired of the regularity of the music, coming at that one hour. Yet there are people who stay here the whole winter. I grow tired of them, and sit in my room.

A letter from my pet, lying on the table, is waiting for me. Very long and full of news. I shall paste it in this place.

"MY OWN DEAREST,—God in his infinite mercy be thanked and praised, for the delightful news each one of your dear letters brings us. Such unhoped-for blessings from Homburg, and, indeed, shall I confess it, when I parted from you, I had a horrid, miserable presentiment, that it was to be the last time I was ever to see that dear face again. I did not let you know the agonies I was suffering. For it was for your own dear health, though I had not the least hope that it would be benefited. But thank God that it is so. Now I shall say no more on that.

"How charming, how amusing, how interesting is your diary, dearest! I have read no novel that comes near to it for interest. So acute, so full of observation, such a knowledge of human character. It brings the whole scene before me; those dreadful people, and that terrible play. And what a picture! It comes back on me at nights in dreams, and I see distorted faces, and the agonies of the poor creatures. And to think of these wicked, cruel men fattening on the innocent! Such life and character—it is *too* graphic! That figure of the tight-faced man walking about is a portrait, and so is that of that cold-blooded Mr. D'Eyncourt. I have read it over two or three times to our little darlings, at least the portions they are likely to understand, and they laughed so. Mr. Barnard, our dear friend and benefactor, was greatly amused, and said in a joking way, we should see you turning gambler yourself, you were so violent against them. He took their part, and said they were no worse than a

13—2

registered society—just like any of our railway or banking companies who took the
money of widows and orphans, and there
was nothing said about it.

"But oh, how strange, how wonderful
your meeting Grainger. Poor Grainger! I
suppose I may call him now. *Indeed* I am
sorry, and you can tell him so from me, for
I have much to reproach myself about him.
I was very foolish then, and thought that
amusing myself with gentlemen was the
most entertaining thing in the world, as
you said once to me, 'having a number of
their scalps hanging at my waist.' Do tell
him I hope he has quite forgotten.

"*Dearest, I write the above for you to show
to him. Do not, I conjure you, offend him
in any way, for I know, which you cannot
know, he never has forgiven me, nor ever will
forgive me. I saw enough of him to know*

that he is vindictive; and indeed he threatened, the very last interview, that he would live to punish you, and *me*, through you. This, indeed, is making me most uneasy, and I do wish he was not there, or you away. But there is only a short time more, thank Heaven; so be very kind to him, or if you see that is no good, keep him at a distance."

My poor little Dora! What a wonderful head it has—peopled with nightmares. Let me point out to her the inconsistency of her previous little advice. She said:

" Be very kind to him," and yet I am to "keep him at a distance." She must send me a recipe for this mysterious double duty; for, for the life, I don't know how to begin it. There is a smack of the country-town in it; but I am afraid, for the world, its little advice is not of the soundest. Dearest, *affection* is your strong point, outside that charmed circle, I am afraid—but I wont say any more.

"Mr. Barnard joins me in this warning, and, strange to say, came back later, very serious. He says that everything that you have written about Grainger bears out what I fear. The man is trying to get an influence over you for ends of his own. He says it is transparently clear, and is going to write to you himself to be on your guard. He has seen more of the world, dearest, and, as I say, he has entirely based his opinion *on some little points, which he says* '*were unconsciously revealed*' *in your diary.*"

Now, here again I must pause to give a little lecture to my Dora. This history was meant entirely for her own gentle eyes; in it I unfold my most secret thoughts and speculations. I confess I did *not* think it would be exhibited to Mr. Barnard, benefactor as he is of mine, and as I must still

call him. Through every mind are coursing
the strangest inconsistencies, wishes, plans,
ideas, which one would be ashamed to admit the existence of to any one, save to the
dearest. *Outwardly* the wise man will not
let such interior feelings affect his actions.
So in future, I really trust my darling
wont exhibit my nonsense to *any* one, especially as it has brought me into discredit
with Mr. Barnard, who, you see, has formed
already rather a low opinion of my strength
of mind. I am sorry he thinks so poorly
of me, yet he is welcome indeed. For
never, *never* can I forget the kindness he
has loaded me with. He has saved my life,
and saved our little home; for I shall return strong and healthy, please God. Still
he does not know me, nor to what a discipline I have subjected myself all my life.
It does amuse me—though others might be
provoked—to see the air of superiority

mankind loves to take. There is no more complacent shape of vanity than is found in the speech—"I know more than *you*." I am *sure* Barnard thinks I am some poor inefficient being. It is not for me to convict him of folly, or indeed of being wrong.

CHAPTER XIX.

WHAT oddities there are in these various
foreign countries, and nothing more odd
here than this. Homburg itself is quite
Protestant, with about fifty Catholics or so;
yet we walk across a few fields and we
come upon a purely Catholic little village
called Kirdorff, in which it is said there is
not a single Protestant. In another direc-
tion three miles off, there is a village as
purely Huguenot, composed entirely of
French Protestants, who talk in some mysterious compound of old French and German. These, I say, seem what a precise
English friend called "quite refreshing

ethnological eccentricities." From Kirdorff
comes news that a German archbishop is to
preach and confirm on Sunday. It was a
pleasant walk in the fresh air of a morning
that seemed to hide its face coquettishly
under a thin veil, and whisper " By-and-by
you will see my face in all its splendour."
A queer little German village of thick raw
reds and greens, which are so uncomfortable
to look at; good houses built of very rude
bricks and framework, but a really fine
church with two tall spires. In this little
spot, whose street winds and turns a great
deal, they have tried in their honest simple
way to do honour to their visitor. There
are green triumphal arches of fir, sur-
mounted each with a cross, and every house
is festooned with green garlands of fir.
The whole town was literally gathered into
this handsome church, and not a head was
in any window; the men at one side, grim,

rather gaunt creatures, and the women at the other. It had all the air of a little village festival—innocent, pretty, fervent— with the rows of young girls in white and flowers, waiting for confirmation. Now the Archbishop, a tall figure with a good massive head, is preaching with extraordinary earnestness, and gestures and tones .which are really new and dramatic, and which at home might enliven some of our sermons. Then the rude German voices are raised in their favourite hymns, given out with stentorian power, moving slowly and lumberingly, but still with fine effect. I cannot but think that the gang of money-changers yonder, whose rival temple I can see from the porch, if they were driven out, as they shortly will be, would not scruple to set up their infamous wheels and tables in this sacred precinct, should no other place be found. The contrast was indeed

wonderful; but I am a little staggered by
seeing next me a very notorious croupier,
with his little boy, and a hymn-book in his
hand.   The respectable name of "the
Bank" I suppose has blinded him.   I am
glad to see all the carriages in Homburg
have driven out to this function at Kirdorff,
and I can make out at the top some fair
English girls who do not belong to that
fold, but who look on with a gentle interest and respectful attention.   There is a
little "stereoscopic slide" for my pet.

CHAPTER XX.

THERE are certain things going on about me here which amaze me. I am of course not surprised at anything here—for I was prepared for much: and I knew that the very *drainage* of Europe oozed through this place. From the dirty offscourings of Europe—mean foreign men, and animal women, I could expect nothing special. But I have always held that our own brave nation—our pure Englishwomen, and even pure Englishmen—who use baths, and honest hunting, and field sports, were the "good boys" and monitors of the Great European school. I am sorry, nay shocked, to see that this notion must soon pass away. Our Englishmen of rank, as a body, are held to be true gentlemen, and whatever their failings in private, they have had a precious sense of decency. A faith that was immovable in the duty of their station, to do no single act that would sully their coronation robe, or rust their coronet. (Barnard, or whoever sees this, will of course say this is "fine writing." But whatever comes of these rough notes, I am determined to set down honestly, and as forcibly as I can, what I think, and what I think of all I see.) There is many a long column in many a newspaper, which describes these things with an indulgent reprobation, a sort of relishing and secretly admiring description. Those who read are invited rather than repelled. They must earn their crust, they will say. But at what an *awful* discount! The terrible responsi-

bility would appal me! I think they ought
to starve. Think of their dying moments,
when these foolish light words shall come
rushing back on them; when the money is
spent, the crust eaten, and the fatal Bill is
presented to be taken up. Already the
wretched souls of those whom their light
words have tempted and destroyed, are mus-
tering along the fatal roadside to curse and
demand vengeance. No, let us have nothing
mealy-mouthed. Let our clergy speak out
as boldly as I do. Not that I blame them
so much—" 'tis their nature to"—they grow
mole-eyed from not using their eyes and
wits, and jogging on in the old rut, and in
the old cart they use for a pulpit. Again,
do I think, if I had taken that course, how
much I should have done! Am I eloquent?
Yes. What vanity! No. Let me tell
you earnestness is eloquence, Messrs. Barnard and Bulmer; wish a thing heartily,

and it will make you eloquent.   Be indifferent, and though you have the tongue of a
Chrysostom——

I say, if I wore a surplice, and preached
of a Sunday, would it not be my duty to
denounce, in the most scathing language I
could command, the scandal that is acted
in high places.   There is an English personage here,—ducal, portly, who is here
I know not why—scarcely for one end.
I do blush for him: and more for the
sickly toadyism of our newspapers and
their correspondents, who dare not call attention to the scandal.   At home, this man
is great in office, has patronage, and I believe is particular as to the " Service" which
he directs, and its conduct.   On a breach
of morals he would be " down," as the slang
goes.   Every one at home believes him to
be a portly, · good humoured, tolerably
honest English nobleman, a little German

in his notions, but sound at the core. He
had sown an acre or so of wildish oats—
who, in his position, had not done that?

But what do we see here? an unblushing
outrageous exhibition, and I cannot but
think if it was known at home there would
be some noise—the virtuous public would
take it up. A very ordinary lady, mature
in years, mature in colour, Mrs. ——, ap-
pears every morning and evening, and is
paid assiduous court to. Out wandering
over the innocent hills, breathing the balmy
airs, we meet the hired carriage, and the
same conventional " happy pair," and almost
wish for Peter Pindar to be " redivivus"
again, and he would be as facetious on this,
as he was on the royalty of his day. This
elderly Colin and Amanthis is too good.
More, there is an ancient battered hench-
man in attendance on the personage, who
seems to fetch and carry; his duty is to

recruit the dinner each day, whip up the doubtful lordling, and the more doubtful ladyling; make up the half dozen or so at the kursaal. These have all not so many "handles" to their names, so the vulgar phrase goes, as stories. This one separated from his wife—that one, "she had a curious affair with Lord ——; but there was some sort of explanation, you know."

There, I hear my dear say, "O how wicked! how you lash these people, and so satirically. I shall be so afraid after all this!" Poor little soul, I daresay you never thought I had this in me, no more than, I daresay, did Mr. Barnard, or the poor creature Bulmer. I daresay there are other gifts in me which you, dear, don't so much as dream of. This, however, I begin to feel every hour yet more strongly: that it was an ill fate that consigned me to a country-town, to a bank office; I should have had greater and wider space wherein to stretch my arms, to breathe. I was made to deal with, to encounter, men, to pierce into their motives, to tear off shams.

Vanity, self-confidence! our friends Barnard and Bulmer will repeat. So it would seem to a hundred like them, for such do not see below the surface. Thoughtful men of the world begin to understand that a certain assertion, an outspoken belief in yourself, is not to be confounded with vanity.

CHAPTER XXI.

I MUST repeat here, that for me this going down every day to a fresh table d'hôte is like going out to the play; I feel like Balzac, studying the great comedy of human nature. Plays, indeed, are certain to pall, they are now so poorly written; but the great drama of human life is ever new and inexhaustible.

It just requires a little tact and instinct to pick out the likeliest situation. Sometimes, indeed, I leave it to pure chance, and even then that true instinct helps me unconsciously. There is a way, too, in making the play begin—an art; otherwise with the best materials the actors refuse to act. I am often amused at the clumsy way in which our countrymen try and break conversational ground—showing that they *want* to talk for talking's sake—a proceeding, of course, resented—and the curtain refuses to rise. There is quite another way of doing it. You shall hear.

Yesterday I find myself beside a lady with a widow's cap—tall, and with finely cut features, and who must have been very handsome in her youth. She was by herself I could see, and there was an air of interest and satisfaction that showed either that the world was excellently well with her, or that she had very little interest in the world at all. (This may seem a paradox to my pet, or perhaps unintelligible, but it is a curious and refined distinction.) Very soon we were talking away, or rather I made her talk away. She told me all about herself: she was Mrs. Arthur Paget, widow of a Colonel Paget, who had died abroad, leaving her with an only son, Arthur. She had been an heiress, and all her money was to go to her only child and son Arthur. There, the stop was drawn out, and on that key she began to play, and played finely and with enthusiasm. I knew in a moment where her heart and treasure was. He was grown up, about one-and-twenty, and only a month before she had made over to him all her money, save a small portion sufficient for herself. He was the finest, noblest, bravest, handsomest fellow in existence; and, she added, doated on her. "All his dear heart is in me," she said, "as of course mine is in him; though that is nothing, and one does not balance the other. He worships the ground I walk on, he says, and would do anything I wished. I would have gladly given him everything I possessed in the world, and been dependent on him, for everything he had would be mine, and indeed I would rejoice to be dependent on him. But my dear boy would not hear of it."

This was their first trip together abroad. They enjoyed everything. It was all new, charming, rapturous. Everything glittered and sparkled; everything was good and kind and obliging. How well I knew this strain; it always flows from the *débutante* tourist.

" Is he in ill health ?" I asked, gravely; " are you in ill health ? Some physician has ordered the waters, I suppose ?"

" Dear, no," she said—" God forbid! He is as healthy as he is handsome. A finer specimen of a boy you could not see, and as innocent as a child—no softness, observe, for he is wide awake, as the slang goes."

" This is not the place, I fear, for the

innocent to come to—it takes the bloom off such an article sadly."

" Oh, I do not look below the surface," she answered, coldly ; " we take things here as we find them. My child would walk through the most dangerous places without raising his eyes, save to look round for me. Besides, I wish him to learn a little life, to mix more, and make acquaintances. But he says, poor boy, he asks nothing beyond me, his poor old mamma."

" He must be quite a phœnix," I said, smiling. " I shall be curious to see him."

" And I should be glad that you should, and know him also. I have noticed you, and some one was speaking about you, that you had done some good here."

This I disclaimed. I have the wish, and, in my trifling way and tiny circle, would do anything I could; but Heaven knows that is not much.

So they begin to talk of my little missionary work, such as it is. Well, it is a sign of something. Well, all I say is, wait; only give me a little time. Perhaps we shall have M. D—— coming to me from the gambling firm, with an offer of a large sum down, to go away. That would be a triumph. What would I answer, though? No indignant "spurning," no foolish warmth; a simple, straightforward reply, from one man of the world and of business, to the other. "My good M. D——, excuse me, you have mistaken your man—*I am an Englishman, not a Frenchman.*" That would be thrust the first. "This is a matter that cannot be compromised. What I do is not from any personal spite to you and to your company, but a holy duty. Let me but have strength, and light, and aid from above, and I shall wage an eternal war against you and yours unto the death. Further, be

prepared for this,—I shall return here again
and again, lift up my voice, protest, until
this frightful leprosy is extirpated. Please
give that as my answer to your firm."

How he would stare! Frenchman as he
is, he would be thrown back, as it were.
How he would shrug and caper to his fellows in their den!

The youth was gone, his mother told me,
to join a little party into Frankfort. He
was very reluctant to go, but she had insisted. " I am determined," she said, " he
shall amuse himself and learn to be a man.
Why should he be tied to the side of his
mother?"

" One of the best restraints he could have,"
I answer, gravely; " it will be relaxed soon
enough, never fear."

After dinner, walking about through the
pleasant grounds, listening to the delicious
music, I see both mother and son sitting

together. He scarcely deserved all her raptures, though he was a fresh, girlish, pink-faced boy, abounding certainly in health and spirits. He seemed overflowing with happiness, and enjoyment of this world so new to him. Every moment I could see his eyes turned to her with something like adoration. It was certainly something strange and curious to me, to see, in the centre of this hotbed of corruption, so innocent a flower blooming away like a tropical plant. It was a most dramatic contrast; and yet, had I been his mother, with the influence she professed to have, I certainly would not have introduced him there. We are told that those who love the danger, have a certain end before them.

She beckoned to me.

"Arthur," she said, "I want you to know this gentleman, who has been giving me some very good advice about you."

The foolish woman!

"I should not presume," I began——

"No," she went on; "there should be no secrets between mother and son. What I hear, he hears at the same moment. He says we should not have come to this place. Now, as to that, what do you say?"

"I say what you say, mother." And he looked at her with an inexpressible affection.

I was a little provoked. This was nursery like—very much to be admired in its way, but alas! would not do for this world. Just as feasting on poetry books will not get a man on at the bar, this sort of exuberant confidence in oneself was surely tempting fate.

"No," she went on, smiling in triumph, "Arthur and I are together a match for the world and all its arts. Against each, singly, they *might* prevail. What do you say, my darling? But against us both——"

His answer was given out of his eyes.

It was hard not to be touched by such affection. After all, affection, like faith, may remove mountains, and may oppose successfully even avalanches. But still, darling Dora of mine, my old hobby comes prancing up. Too much self-confidence is a challenge, as it were. It invites attack, where less obtrusiveness would escape notice.

I sat down beside them. After all, I hate the *rôle* of professional lecturer or monitor. Much more may be done by a little insinuation of good, rather than by a direct homily *à la* Bulmer. I set myself out to interest and amuse them, pointing out the notabilities, and introducing stories about the fatal scabies, or the leprosy of the place.

" It is the strangest thing," I said, " how familiarity blunts us to everything. We all of us know the nicest, most moral people, who, if they were told, 'that money I now put into your hand was taken from some unfortunate wretches, who first starved, and then in despair committed suicide'—would surely fling it down in horror and disgust. This may be exceptional—the suicide, I mean; but more certain still is the beggaring, the wrecking of domestic households, and worse again, the wreck of many a soul. This is no speculation—these are facts, repeating themselves every hour of the day. And yet you will see English ladies and gentlemen coming away from these tables chuckling over the gold and silver in their hands, their winning of which will cause the miseries I have described."

They seemed actually scared. A sketch of a few touches is often more effectual than a whole elaborate picture. I am so full of the awful force of this scourge, that such vigorous etching comes from me naturally, and without effort.

I was content "to leave it there," as the phrase runs.

I pointed them out D'Eyncourt and Grainger—the potentate—the great gambling Count, who was all the time being drawn by invisible strings towards destruction—with his indifferent interest in the music, &c. I knew the man was acting. Oh, there are many rude, coarse words popular in the odious slang of our time; but I cannot quarrel with that dubbing of a gaming house "a hell;"—most appropriate, and not too highly coloured a title.

The lady seemed to know something about Grainger, and you may be sure, dearest, that I smiled as she said she heard " he had been crossed in some attachment."

She asked, too, had he "not been badly treated?" Rogue Dora! I daresay he had. I said it was possible. I did give them a short sketch of what I knew about him, enlisting I believe their sympathies. The young fellow said he was handsome, and " appeared to have seen a great deal of life." I could not help replying out, with a smile—

" Do you know what 'seeing a great deal of life' means in its conventional shape? Owing large sums of money— ruining your health—ruining other people —destroying your own sense of pure enjoyment—destroying your chance of future happiness; in short, *injuring* yourself in every way; *that* is seeing a good deal of life! I fancy, Mrs. Paget, it would be better on the whole *not* to see a good deal of life on such terms."

She reflected a moment and looked very

grave. But then brightened and said, "Oh, but he must enjoy himself, and I promised him! And indeed I would not like them to say he was tied to—— Though," she added, smiling, "mothers have long since given up wearing aprons and strings."

"Rather," I answered, "they are snapped over and over again."

My pet will own to me without fear of making me vain, that since I came to this place, there has developed in me a vein for repartee and of readiness, which I own surprises me. I take no pride in such a gift, Heaven knows, but it might have lain till my death in that mean country-town of ours, undiscovered—undreamed of, like a pot of old coins in the ground.

The youth had been looking at her affectionately. He caught her shawl—"This will do as well as an apron-string," he said, "and be much stronger too."

I felt a great interest in this pair and in their almost pastoral innocence—the looks of unspeakable affection they now and again gave at each other.

"Ah," she said, "if our dear friend—his darling father, were now with us, how he would enjoy this!—such happy days as we had together. He made everything happy. All he cared for in life was to be with us. He was a brother to him, rather than a father. And yet no one knew life better. He knew it only to despise it."

We may have remained silent for a moment. In such a place, in such an atmosphere, it was refreshing to meet such almost holy feelings, though there was a discordance. "He would have told you," I said, gently, "the dangers of such a place as this, and his firm paternal voice would warn against that fatal pitfall yonder—that hideous crevasse which is concealed with the loveliest flowers."

"Oh, the tables!" he said.

"Yes," she said, "those dreadful tables! He had a horror of even cards."

"The tables," I said, "exactly! That is the gentle name they go by. A vile gambling hell would not do for ears polite, or the euphuism that custom and their little attentions to ladies has purchased. Why in the days of Crockford's there was always a supper—champagne; the whole supplied in the handsomest manner gratis. A glass of their wine would be like poison to me."

"You are indeed right," she said. "It is a shocking place. It terrifies me sometimes; and only Dr. M'Kee sent us here for the waters —— He *really* did, and for *him*."

"To be sure," I said, "and Sir Duncan Dennison sent me. We are not to be deprived of innocent blessings; and if a gracious Providence strikes the rock and lets a health-giving stream spout up to cure

15—2

our ills, we are not to be kept from it because a gang of ruffians choose to encamp under the trees close by. You are justly astonished at my using such a word in speaking of the good-natured, affable gentlemen who are doing so much to amuse us all here and make things pleasant. But why indulge in these complacent hypocrisies? I make no secret of it; from the hour I arrived here I laid myself out to call things by their right names—to strip off their gilt washing, and unfold what I know to be conventional lies—yes, lies, in the face of that heaven there. Is it possible that decent, respectable, religious people can suppose, when they come here, that they are to abdicate all the responsibility they have at home? If there was a low gambling place in some of those purlieus of the Haymarket, would any English matron be seen going into it with her daughters? No, no, my dear Mrs. Paget, there is no use compromising these matters. Because there are gilded rooms, and servants, and lords and genteel people walk in and look on, we are not the less responsible. The more respectable we are, the more our respectable sanction contributes to the wreck and ruin of the miserable victims of the system. There are people here, who will tell you this is all ridiculous, and they may laugh at *me*, but I cannot, quixotic as it may seem, look on at what I think SIN—sin in all its bearings, colour, size—no matter how you look at it. I speak warmly, I know, and perhaps stand alone, but I am genuine, and feel what I say."

"You have put it in a way that I never thought of before," she said, reflecting.

It is indeed a responsibility. He, too, was looking at me with wonder. It had struck *his* boyish mind. I am convinced if our preachers and men like Bulmer, were to put their truths in more common shape, and take the measure, as it were, of the minds they were addressing, and shape their speech accordingly, it would have the happiest effect. I determined to leave the matter as it was, but I knew I had made an impression, and was content. I then changed the subject.

CHAPTER XXII.

Saturday.—I am getting more and more entertained every hour with the spectacle here. Again I repeat there would seem to be no such dramatic touchstone to bring out human nature and human character. If one had but a window in every forehead! The strangest thing is the utter ignorance and wildness of these poor dupes, who play on without principle or approach to system. It is all so simple, so easily attainable, and yet it occurs to no one. This morning *I win eight times in succession.* In spirit I mean. I paste the card in here as a little relic, and as a proof of my fore-

casting powers.   The marks show when I
played—I mean in spirit.   .

R.	N.	R.	N.
•			
	•		•
•	•		•
•		•	
•		•	
	•		•
	•	•	
	•		
•			•
•	•	•	

My pet will see this at a glance, that the
two colours really alternate in equal batches.
Had I been one of the players—just to give
you an idea of the easy way the money is
made—I should have earned enough in ten
minutes to have paid all our year's rent.

This morning, when we were all doing
our procession at the wells, that agreeable

man of God, the Dean of ——, comes up to
me, with that smug obsequiousness which
he has unconsciously got to exhibit to infe-
riors, from the habit of always addressing
lords and baronets.

"I saw your name," he said, "in the
Fremdenliste, and at once thought you
must be one of the Edward Austens of Berk-
shire.   Am I right—the member?"

"Yes," I said; "my father was Edward
Austen, the member."

"Good gracious! I was sure of it.   How
wonderful are the ways"—he was going to
add "of Providence!" but more decorously
substituted, "the ways—ahem—we find
people turning up!"

Of course he had not heard of my fall in
the world, or, if he had, thought it was one
of those genteel bits of ruin which don't
affect people of condition.   He was a great
man at a charity sermon, and very strong

"against Rome." We walked up and down together, he chattering all the time, with every now and again a nod and "How d'ye do?" to some one. After which he would get abstracted, and look after the lord uneasily—I think meditating whether there was likely to be a vacancy beside the lord, when *he* might join in. I remember a sermon by this dignitary of extraordinary warmth and power, on the text, "Go up higher," which, in his own life, he illustrated forcibly; and I believe the true bearing for him of the text was unconsciously this: "he that humbleth himself" was to do so through the hope of being exalted. I dare say I do him wrong in this, for he was a charitable man; but certainly loved a lord a little too much. He asked me "to make one of their party" at dinner at the "Shepherdess," a mean, obscure place, which some irreverent people always called "that pot-house of a place," but where "the swells" were fond of planning dinners. Is not this the world all over! Some obscure spot or thing is taken up by "ladies of quality"— no matter what discomfort or stupidity follows, the world pronounces it *charming*, and would give their poor battered souls— and cheapest thing they have—to get there.

I went to the Shepherdess that evening, and found ten people at the dean's table. Only one lord—the salt of the earth—but certainly some "nice people," as he would call them. The dinner was bad enough, as, indeed, Mr. Boxwell, a hearty jovial member of parliament, said plainly.

"In fact, my dear dean, what surprises me altogether is to find you in this queer place at all."

"Find me here," repeated the dean— "find me here! Surely there are the nicest people—Lord ——, Lady ——, and

Sir John; why, there is nothing queer about *them*."

"I don't mean that; but I was thinking of a sermon I have heard of yours, on 'Responsibility,' and all that, and how one preached more by simply not saying a word, than by regular sermons. A capital idea, by the way, which I wish was carried out in all our churches."

"Oh, that's all very well," said the dean.

(I know these conversations amuse my pet, and I try to recollect scraps of them as nearly as possible.)

"In short, it is so droll," went on the member, "to find the good people gathered here—aprons, shovels, white ties, gaiters, high collars, holy faces—all clustered about a common gambling-house. You can call it Kursaal, and all that, and talk of the croupier and such dignified names; but we know, if the great Blanc himself took a scrubby room in St. James's street, the police would just burst in, and drag him and his croupiers with unnecessary violence before Sir Thomas Henry, who would refuse bail."

I enjoyed this thoroughly. These are my own views, only put so much better. But the dean was a shrewd man, and when he saw we were all listening, said: " Oh, we come for our healths. We are ordered here, sir. Our health. Those people, you know, have nothing to do with me. And, to tell you the truth, I don't look at it in your way at all. They tell me it is all perfectly fair and above board; and I *hear* the good they do, the sums they give away in charity, is something incalculable! The widows and the orphans of the place come to them, and never go away empty."

I was astonished to hear such careless language from a man in so responsible a position, and could not resist saying, " But how many a widow and orphan, Mr. Dean, have they made destitute? How many households have they filled with desolation? The ruin they have caused spreads over every land, and many and many are the dismal messengers they have dismissed to English homes with hopeless news. Is the wretched alms, which they are *forced* to pay, any compensation for this wholesale pillage?"

I spoke warmly, and the dean looked round at me with disgust. " That is all very good and sound, and we are all agreed, of course: but we must take things as we find 'em. These people found out the wells here, and worked 'em, and developed 'em. If I was inclined to a little sophistry or casuistry, I would ask you, wouldn't the myriads of rheumatic and dyspeptic fathers whom they have restored to health—the thousands of wasting daughters to whose cheeks the what-d'ye-call-'em —Le Wheez'un Broonin"—so he pronounced it—" has brought back colour; the number of homes it has made happy—is not all this a sort of compensation for the weak-minded, ridiculous gambler, whom they justly punish? And serve 'em right too. Now, sir?"

"That's putting it very well, dean," said the member, laughing; "and, if I don't mistake, Mr. Austen has benefited amazingly himself by the gambling waters."

"Oh dear, yes," said the dean; "there is quite too much cant about all this. We must take 'em as we find 'em. My stockbroker, a worthy man, gives money to schools, holds plates, and all that—but he gambles on the Exchange, and wins; and who does he win from? From some one who has to lose his all to pay him. He made a hundred thousand pounds in Italian stock the other day. How? Some poor wretch sold in the panic, and was destroyed. Well. My broker bought *his* stock. Look at the merchants. Look at Lord ——, who made the last bishop, why, *he* games on the turf. My good sir, if we're to go about setting right everything we see or *think* wrong, why the world might as well stop. We might all shut up. We must give and take."

Is not this characteristic? An ordained man—a dean—and I, a poor, unauthorized, unaccredited being, obliged to tell him *his* duty!

I was indignant to hear such indifference from one in his sacred position—no heart, no earnestness; and I answered, warmly: "But, Mr. Dean, when we see this place crowded with holy—I mean with officially holy—men, is there not something more expected than giving and taking? What do we hear? Not a word, not a protest, not a denunciation of the wickedness going on about us; no thunderings from the pulpit. I cannot understand it. Surely, if we could suppose a Whitfield, or a Wesley, or a John Knox, or a Luther, or a Calvin, were found here——"

"Heaven forbid!" said the member of parliament. "The place would get too hot for me! Come, we have had enough of this wine and of the Shepherdess; and to show that I quite approve of the dean's good sense, I am going up to the gambling-rooms now, to try what can be done with a napoleon."

As we went out the dean spoke to me very testily, as if he were sore, and wincing under my thrust.

" See here. You are a little too high-flying, my friend," he said, "and not exactly cut out for a reformer. Believe me, there is no harm in following the general *consensus* of leading men. You see all the distinguished personages here, lay and clerical, neither protest nor approve. They go their own way. Joshua was the only one who succeeded in stopping the sun. Above all, let us look at home, and keep a guard over ourselves. While you are busy giving directions, and helping the old ladies across the street, saving them from the omnibuses, you yourself may be run over."

And these are the pastors for the poor sheep of England; smooth words to make everything comfortable, and macadamize the road to salvation. This man is sure to be a bishop. Well, I shall say no more after *this*. He has taken no notice of me since.

CHAPTER XXIII.

Monday the sixth. — The more I look about me in this strange world, and certainly in this strangest of places, the more do I feel that it is good for me *morally* to be here. For my weak, but well-meaning soul, it has the effect of bracing, nerving, cold water. I shall return home strengthened and invigorated. I am not at all sorry to have passed by these furnaces without being scorched. The man who shuts himself up and turns away his eyes is discreet, and if he knows himself to be weak, all is right. Nay, a greater authority than I has written, he is *bound* to gird himself up, and flee as fast as his poor tottering limbs can carry him. If I were a clergyman—a supposition I very often make, and there *was* some talk of it when I was a boy —I would ascend my pulpit, and preach eternally on this text. If you feel a spark of courage and strength, *face* the danger cautiously, practise, do as a man does who goes to a gymnasium and trains his muscles —begin to throw a half stone weight, and increase the amount by degrees. I would thunder this at the congregation until they began to think it was a monomania, as I daresay she, whose eyes will be reading this by-and-by, may herself think. Or with more indulgence she will perhaps say, "My dear, I have heard Dr. Bulmer preach far worse." Well, perhaps he has, and I shall be told I have no business to be dressing myself up in a surplice—*en amateur.* But I say again this does me good, and it

will do me good again to read it, and perhaps years hence strange eyes will fall upon
it, and reflect, and own, perhaps a little
reluctantly, "Well, he is the first that has
got sermons, not out of stones, which would
be a limited range of subject, but out of
roulette and the card-table, and the wolfish
eyes of 'hell keepers.'" There, darling, I
wont preach again until further notice.

But the truth is, I am in a sort of elation, for I did more than mere rapid preaching this day. Speech may be silvern, silence
golden, but *action* is, after all, a diamond.
Going in this night to the roulette table, I
see an unusual crowd, and faces showing
that stupid interest and admiration which
is about as sincere as that of the crowd
who stand gaping at the foolhardy Blondin
or the reckless Leotard. Fifty per cent. of
that crowd has a lingering and secret aspi-
ration that if a catastrophe *were* to be, they

might be only present to see it. Here I
find they are staring at a tall gay Englishman, a fresh good-looking fellow in some
regiment, and whose honest health and loud
proclamation of the tub every morning,
contrasts with the yellow, dirty faces and
the niggardly economy of soap, linen, &c.,
which *they* insinuate. His play is of the
boldest, not laying the table broadcast with
his gold as some foolish ones do; but with
a sort of instinct selecting a number here,
another there, and "bedding and potting"
it, as some one said, with his gold. What
I delight in is his contemptuous treatment
of the crew of croupiers, whom he treats
as though they were mere scavengers or
nightmen, not fit to be addressed, or as
you would a dependant. He tosses them
his money insolently, and makes them
arrange it for him, and if they are awk-
ward, speaks to them with a haughty arro-

gance that seems to exasperate them. He
has won with many pieces on Zero, he has
hit the number again and again, and I see
the brigand eyes of the "hell keepers"
glancing at him furtively, with anger and
dislike, as though they were thinking,
"Shall we 'set' him with some of our bullies as he goes home to his hotel, and strip
him of what he has robbed us of?" Ap-
proving faces are bent on this darling,
whom Fortune in one of her caprices dan-
dles for a few seconds in her arms, like
some pretty child, and then allows to drop
on the pavement. The enamelled faces of
the mermaids are turned towards him; and
the rustling of their fins and tail is heard,
as they come swimming round a new prey.

I drew near to him, and could hear him
tell a friend behind, " I must have got more
than a thousand out of them," while a voice
that I know, says, in its accustomed drawl,

"Now is the time then; sack 'em, and you'll have the glory of being the first to break the bank this season."

I knew it seemed intrusive, but I could not resist saying, in a low voice, "Now is the time to retire. Luck always changes."

The soapstone face was stretched round to look. "Oh, Grainger's friend!" he said. "This is the gentleman I was telling you of, who has the wonderful system——"

"I have no system," I said, coolly.

"I was wrong, then, it seems." He went on, "Well, it is the gentleman who preaches against the bank one day, and in behalf of his infallible system the next."

The young fellow was naturally not attending.

"Confound it!" he said, "the luck *is* turning. I have got nothing these last three turns. I'll take his advice, and carry off what I have bagged. Come, and let us count. Here's Grainger. Look here, Grainger, my dear boy!"

It was now about half-past eleven. Soon the mystic proclamation would be heard—" *à la dernière!*" Grainger's eyes sparkled with an unholy fire of envy—possibly of disappointment, for I would not do him wrong—as he looked on the glittering treasure which the other was holding in his hand as though it were so much mould. But he turned to me suddenly—

"Here, Pollock, let me introduce a friend of mine—Mr. Austen, the hero of that little story which your brother knows."

I remembered there was a Captain Pollock in the regiment at *that* time, and I remember, Dora, being ludicrously jealous one night, at your dancing with him.

"Oh, indeed!" said the young fellow who had won. "I recollect. But I tell you what; I'll stand a supper at Chevet's for the whole party—neat meat, neat wines, neat everything. Come, no excuse. The winner pays for all, and we'll count the cash between the courses."

Grainger was delighted. I don't set up to be a Puritan, as you know, Dora, and I always think of that saint with admiration, who used to play cards with a swearing and abandoned crew, and thus gradually acquired an influence over them. There again the complacency creeps out—an almost sacerdotal complacency. Precisely like a saint, am I not?—or Mr. Barnard will say so. But again and again I repeat, this is all for your pretty eyes and my own ugly ones.

I went with them. I often say to myself, " On this day, or on this night, let us have a little festival," when I have been good and deserve it; when I have been otherwise, I assure you I can be very stern and severe to myself. So we sat down and counted the gold, which was close on nine hundred napoleons. I own to a certain wrench and a yearning as I looked at it, and I think the amount of *unconscious* greediness—for we are all animals—in the three faces must have been overpowering. I am not at all ashamed to own this. God knows I don't set up to be superior. Two waiters afar off heard the chink—every ear learns that. They sniffed the dear metal as a vulture does carrion. Hungry gamblers looked up from their drink with ferocious envy. The owner alone was unconcerned.

"Confound the beggars! if I didn't think they'd swindle me, I'd have been as glad to have banknotes."

Here was the supper. D'Eyncourt—who to his other vices adds that of gourmandise —spoke little and eat heartily. I confess to doing the same, and most gratefully do I

owe my thanks to the Providence who has
so restored me as to give me the power of
enjoying moderately such things. What have
I done to deserve these mercies, and not become like one of the worn-out beings who
come here and drink with a faint hope of
miraculously recovering their lost stomachs?

We were very merry, Grainger specially
so, and I suspected that the honest lad had
helped his friend with a handful of what he
had carried off.   But D'Eyncourt's cat-like
eyes fell on me several times, as if he was
about to say something.   I was ready for
him.   He began, in his drawl:

"The more I see of you, Mr. Austen, the
more you become a mystery to me."

I have put down some people before now,
so I thought I would settle *him* before he
went further.

"Well, curiously," I said, "the more I
see of *you*, the less you are a mystery to

me; in fact, the first day I read you like a book."

Pollock laughed loud. "Hit you on the sternum, my boy—and quite right, too, though not very flattering."

"Austen's mauleys come down hard when they do come down," said Grainger.

"What I was saying," said D'Eyncourt, in his slow impressive way (which I *do* envy him), as though he had not heard, or as if he had stopped speaking to light his cigar, which was now all alight—"what I say is, I don't quite understand your *rôle*—I mean the attitude you have to this bank. If I disapproved, *I* should keep away—turn my back on Jericho—let the fiery sword do its work; but I certainly wouldn't shelter myself under their gorgeous roof, sit on their luxurious sofas, read their English newspapers, with such strong convictions. I'd be almost inclined to go to M. Blanc, the head of the thing, and tell him so boldly."

I was not sorry that he had begun in this fashion, and really wished to "tackle" him before them; and I was amused too, for I knew this was what would occur to common minds, and to men like Mr. Barnard.

" I think," said I, smiling, " we can all imagine M. Blanc's polite and pleasant repartee, if any such well-meaning remonstrant were to present himself. But the fact is, I do *not* use their *Times*, or their luxurious sofas and chairs; and as for their roof —well, I do own to taking that barren advantage of them."

" Had you again—on the nob this time, D'Eyncourt," said the youth, who had already taken more wine than fitted him to be a nice judge of such effects.

" Do leave those low boxing metaphors

aside, Mr. Pollock—at least among gentle-men. You may not be in such spirits to-morrow night. But"—he went on, turning to me—"you are not quixotic enough to expect that a still small voice like yours—of course I mean your conscience's—could make itself heard in this Babel! Have you such a sense of comical self-delusion that you can place yourself at that large doorway and turn back the mob of scoun-drels, blackguards, roughs, cheats, jailbirds, lorettes—aye, and even decent men and women—with *your* faint expostulation ? Do you tell us that?"

" No," I said, firmly; and then, as po-litely as I could, " but first of all, suppose it was my whim; am I not as much entitled to have *that*, as any one here ?"

" Scarcely," he said. " As a rule, the gamblers never make themselves ridicu-lous."

"That seems like having *you*, my friend," said the boy to me.

"But apart from mere verbal quibbling," I went on, "at the risk of exposing myself to the suspicion of what is called *cant*—which, of course, is saying something that is *moral, or religious, or improving*——"

"Excuse me. The sayer being neither moral nor religious, *that* becomes cant. And you have saved me the trouble of coming to the point; for I believe that, unconsciously, you are at heart as great a gambler as any of them; and—don't be offended, for we are speaking with charming candour—you know the greatest rock is that air of self-righteousness—'Take heed that ye deceive not yourselves.'"

"Oh, I say, come, no profane quoting here," said the youth, with tipsy gravity.

"There is no profanity," I said, smiling;

"your quotation is not in Scripture !" I was in great vein now, and began to feel myself a match for him. " But supposing, now," I went on, " I succeeded in interposing between two, or one even, and their destruction, why I am foolish enough to think it worth while coming so far for that."

" O ! for Grainger, here?" he sneered. " A brand plucked from the burning? You are the neophyte, it seems, Grainger. Well, there *is* a class of missionary they call 'soupers,' and who have rather a suspicious class of converts. But *you are* genuine, Grainger. You are being brought to see the light, are you not? Seriously," he added, turning to me, " you don't mean to tell us you have touched that rocky ground?"

" Seriously," I replied, impatiently, " I don't care to discuss such topics."

"With all my heart, though I daresay our friend Grainger has been doing a little bit of the new regeneration—the softening of this stony heart. (There is a regular dialect for all that, which I profess myself not quite up to.) I can fancy him saying to you, 'What can I do? I am led on— dragged on. I have good intentions. I was virtuous once, and I would give worlds to be back in the old innocent times—the fields, the green, the buttercups—to be like *you*, in short.' Ha, ha!"

"Ha, ha!" roared the host. "Devilish good."

It *was* so like what Grainger had been saying, that I turned sharply and looked at him with surprise. He was looking at D'Eyncourt with quite a wicked glare.

"There is always some devilish malignity in your ideas, D'Eyncourt," he said—a speech that was certainly just and nicely descriptive. For he might surely guess that I had, in my poor way, and by the grace of one greater than I acting through me, made some impression on Grainger; and this artful ridicule would be precisely a fashion that Satan himself would have suggested for throwing him back.

"Well," said D'Eyncourt, "we've had enough. Let us go in and see these honest fellows counting their money. I hope they have got a good bag to-night; they work hard enough for it—harder than many a fellow at home on his sixpence a day, and deserve every coin they get. Good luck to them! I hope they've emptied many a fool's pocket."

As we went out Grainger whispered, "You don't mind what that snarler says.

He'd sneer at his dead mother. I'm bad enough, God knows——"

"Don't say a word, Grainger," I said, taking his arm; "his speeches will have very little effect on me."

END OF VOL. I.

www.ingramcontent.com/pod-product-compliance
Lightning Source LLC
Chambersburg PA
CBHW020354030726

47496CB00007B/2129